A JIGGY McCUE STORY

MURDER &CHIPS

MICHAEL LAWRENCE

ORCHARD

ORCHARD BOOKS
338 Euston Road, London NW1 3BH
Orchard Books Australia
Level 17/207 Kent Street, Sydney, NSW 2000

First published in the UK in 2012 by Orchard Books

ISBN 978 1 40831 396 1

A CIP catalogue record for this book is available from the British Library.

1 3 5 7 9 10 8 6 4 2

Printed in Great Britain

Orchard Books is a division of Hachette Children's Books,
an Hachette UK company.

www.hachette.co.uk

For the ever-inspired and inspiring
Sarah Jane Perry

THE CAST

Jiggy McCue, a boy
Angie Mint, a girl
Pete Garrett, another boy
Peg McCue, a mother
Mel McCue, a father
Audrey Mint, another mother
Oliver Garrett, another father
Roderick Basket-Case, an organiser
Larry Bogart, a butler
Gerald Tozer, a guest
Belinda Prosser, another guest
Billy Prosser, Belinda's husband
Sir Duff Naffington, owner of Naffington Hall
Lady Helga Naffington, Sir Duff's wife
Honor Naffington, Sir Duff and Lady H's daughter
Rudy Bollinger, Honor's smarmy boyfriend
Myrtle, a maid
Mona, another maid
Silas Blackthorn, a gardener
Inspector Qwerty, a policeman
Sergeant Fawkes, another policeman
DCI Smurfit, a policewoman

CHAPTER ONE

'What you need,' my mother said, 'is a nice juicy murder. That should take your mind off the exams.'

A bit extreme, wouldn't you say? But you don't know that woman.

I'd been studying for weeks (which really goes against the grain, believe me) and I was pretty stressed out. So were Pete and Angie, my best buds from across the road. It didn't help that everyone kept banging on about how important these exams were if we wanted a rat in hell's chance of any kind of future. Bad enough having to grow up, without the *Future* hanging over us.

'Whatever's in there,' I said, rapping my knuckles on my mother's forehead when she voiced the nice juicy murder thought, 'it can stay there. You and your fruitcake ideas. Look what you've done to Dad.'

What she'd done to Dad was tell him he needed therapy.

'THERAPY?' he'd shouted when he heard this. 'WHAT FOR?'

9

'Mel,' Mum said, ultra-calmly, 'you need to learn how to relax.'

'RELAX? I'M PERFECTLY RELAXED!'

'Come down off the ceiling and say that,' she cooed. 'You're as tense as a coiled spring.'

'TENSE? ME? YOU DON'T KNOW WHAT YOU'RE TALKING ABOUT!'

'You used to just get agitated when your football team lost,' she said, 'but these days you get steamed up about the number of panel games on TV, and custard not being what it was when you were a boy.'

'WELL, DOESN'T *EVERYONE*!?' he bawled.

'The sister of a member of my drama group specialises in relaxation techniques,' Mum went on. 'Relaxation therapy could really calm you down.'

'I AM NOT GOING TO SOME HEADBAND-WEARING HIPPY THERAPIST!' Dad screamed.

'I'll see if she can fit you in next week,' said Mum.

That's the way things work in our house. Mum suggests something, Dad and I tell her she's talking through her earholes, and next thing we know we're doing it. When Dad started the relaxation therapy he didn't come home waving flowers and drooling with joy, but after a couple of sessions he did seem a tad calmer, and now, even when he screamed at footie on the telly, it was a more controlled kind of screaming, like he was doing it because he felt it went with the territory. And once I caught him sitting cross-legged on the landing, eyes closed, a finger and thumb of each hand joined at the tip like they wished they were holding carrots.

Dad had been attending those sessions for a month when Mum came up with the plan to take my mind off the dreaded exams. Not just *my* mind either.

'It's all fixed,' she said to me, Pete and Angie, who happened to be all together in my house at the time. 'Roderick's got the venue sorted, and Audrey and Ollie are on board. We're all going.'

'Even me,' Dad muttered gloomily from behind his soccer magazine.

'Going where?' I said. 'And who's Roderick?'

'You'll see,' said Mum.

'Dad?' I asked.

He flapped his mag. 'I know nothing.'

'Ask your two,' I said to Pete and Angie.

'On it,' said Ange, throwing Pete at the door.

Pete and Angie live under the same roof as her mum and his dad these days, so dragging the info out of them would be a one-stop op. But my mother was speaking into the phone before they were even off the step. 'Aud,' she said. 'Angie and Pete are coming to quiz you about the you-know-what. Warn Ollie.' She clicked off. 'You've been warned too,' she said to Dad. 'Not a word. Not one *word*.'

Dad got up and left the room. Silently. He knows his place.

Apparently this deal of my mother's was going to be a long weekend. I asked how long.

She smirked. 'Murderously long.'

'What's all this murder stuff you keep going on about?'

She just grinned. 'You'll see.'

Mum arranged for her insane parents to come and look after Swoozie my baby sister and Stallone our cat, and that Friday, a Teachers' Training Day (we hoped they were being trained to do something useful for a change), the seven of us piled into our two cars and headed for this place the Golden Oldies wouldn't tell us anything about. About sixteen hours later (one and a bit actually, but it seemed longer) we drove up this drive between trees and braked in this sort of courtyard in front of a huge old house with a round tower on one corner, and battlements. I'd never been in a house with battlements before. A crumbly old castle, yes, but never a house.

'This is where it's all going to happen,' Mum said as she and Dad and I got out of our car.

'All what?' I asked.

'You'll see. Come along.'

I didn't come along. The only one who did was Audrey Mint, Angie's mum. While my mother banged the big black knocker on the big black front door, I joined Pete and Angie at their car. 'Anything?' I said.

'They're gonna leave us here,' said Angie.

'What?'

'It's a school. We're going to be boarders.'

'Boarders? We're being sent away to school? We'll have to *stay* here?'

'That's what I reckon.'

'You reckon? They haven't exactly said?'

'They don't need to. Female intuition.'

I turned to Pete. 'What about you?'

'I haven't got any.'

'Any what?'

'Female intuition.'

'OK, but why do you think we've been dragged here?'

He shrugged. 'Your guess is as good as mine.'

'I don't have a guess.'

'Exactly.'

'They know,' I said, meaning the dads.

My father and Oliver Garrett (Pete's dad) were hanging back, like they were thinking of doing a runner. We sauntered over.

'All right, we're here now,' I said to them. 'Spill.'

'What, and spoil your mother's moment?' Dad said. 'I wouldn't dare.'

'Are you a man or a mouse?' I said.

'Squeak.'

We looked at Ollie.

'Squeak,' he said.

'Pathetic,' said Pete.

'Yeah,' said I.

'It's a male thing,' said Angie. 'Their sons are the same. Not a backbone between the four of you.'

She spun around and swung her hips towards the house. I tutted. She'd been doing a lot of the hip-swinging thing lately. I kept meaning to remind her that the Angie Mints of this world are not hip-swingers. The way she was going she'd be wearing lipstick and eye shadow any time, and talking to boys not called Pete or Jiggy.

Just as Angie got to the big old gloomy house the door opened. A tall thin gent with a stoop and a handful of spiky hair over each ear stood on the mat. 'Welcome to Naffington Hall!' he boomed, and leaned out and lipped my mother's cheeks, both of them.

Mum introduced Audrey. The tall thin gent kissed her hand. Mum introduced Angie. Angie stepped back, hands behind her, and nodded.

'That'll be Roderick,' said Dad.

'Who's who exactly?' I asked.

'You'll see.'

'Why does everyone keep saying that to me?'

'You'll see.'

'One more time,' I said through clenched teeth, 'and I'll sign those papers for the Unwanted Parents' Home and not visit you.'

Pete spoke up. 'I'm not going any further unless someone tells me this isn't a boarding school.'

His dad laughed. 'Boarding school! Where'd you get that from?'

'Angie.'

'Where'd she get it from?'

'She guessed.'

'Well, she guessed wrongly.'

'So it's not a school.'

'No.'

'And we don't have to stay here.'

'Only for the weekend.'

'It really is just a weekend break then?' I said.

'Yes,' said Ollie. 'One that me and Mel are dreading.'

'With a vengeance,' agreed my dad.

'Come along, you four!' Mum called in this mad sing-song voice. 'Come and meet Roderick and hear about the murders!'

CHAPTER TWO

Me, Angie and Pete had been best mates since Year Zero. We were born about the same time, in the same street. Well, not the street exactly, but you know what I mean. Our old dears used to bump their enormous bellies together and cheer about the trio of brilliant little bundles they were about to spew into the world. From the moment we were born we understood each other. Pete and I understood that Angie was the boss because she was a woman. Angie and I understood that Pete was a moron who only thought of his stomach. Pete and Angie understood that I, Jiggy McCue, would be the smartest, handsomest person in the universe the moment I got the hang of hypnotism. We called ourselves The Three Musketeers. If there'd been four of us it might have been something else, but when you're only three, somehow you have to be The Three Musketeers, it's a sort of law. And because we were The Three Musketeers we had to have a battle cry, and the one we came up with (I don't know who to blame for it, but I'm admitting nothing) was

'One for all and all for lunch'. We chanted this all through our childhoods whenever the world blew a raspberry at us. If one of us said 'One for all and all for lunch' the other two had to come running and stand with him or her, with our little chests out and our hands on our hips (though we dropped that when the other kids started to point at us and fall to their knees in hysterics). It was us against the world, see. Always, from the start. We did everything together except go to the toilet. Even went on holiday together. And on long weekends to relieve the stress of Very Important upcoming exams.

'Welcome to Naffington Hall!'

The full name of the tall thin gent who greeted us – the way I heard it anyway – was Roderick Basket-Case. 'This your gaff?' my dad asked him when the intros were history.

'Oh, no,' said Rod B-C. 'I've merely borrowed it for our weekend. It belongs to Sir Duff Naffington. We'll meet him and his family shortly.'

'*Sir* Duff?' whispered Angie to Pete and me. 'We're not supposed to curtsy or anything, are we?'

'I curtsy to no one,' said Pete.

'Have you told the youngsters what it's all about?' Roderick asked Mum.

'No, I thought I'd leave that to you.'

17

He chuckled. 'They're in for a high old time. Come in, everyone, come in!'

We trooped into this huge wood-panelled room – the 'hall', Roderick called it – with a ceiling as far above the floor as the average roof on the Brook Farm Estate, where we live. A brass chandelier dangled on a long chain from above and there was a staircase wide enough for six people to walk up shoulder to shoulder. To our left there was a colossal stone fireplace with high-backed armchairs and couches grouped round it. The fire wasn't lit. A ginormous red rug covered most of the floorboards, and on the walls there were paintings of serious geezers and geezeresses with staring eyes. There was also a big black piano, but not on the wall.

'Wow.'

That was Angie. Her jaw was sagging as she stared around, at the furnishings, the pictures, the chandelier, the size of the place. Pete and I shook our heads. Girls. So easily impressed. 'People have been murdered here and we're spending the weekend to take our minds off the *exams*?' I whispered.

'Seems to be the plan,' said Pete.

'My mother's insane.'

'Old news,' he said.

'There are three other guests,' Roderick told us.

'The last has yet to arrive, but come and meet my niece and her hubby.' He led us through one of the doors off the hall. 'The dining room,' he said.

More armchairs round an unlit fire. Sitting up in one of them, like a guest, was a tatty old book with the words *Latin Names of Common Flowers* on the cover. Arched windows looked out over a rambling garden. Under the windows was a long shiny dining table. Two people sat so close together at the table that they might have been joined at the thigh.

'This is Belinda and Billy,' Roderick said. 'Mr and Mrs Prosser as of two days ago.'

'Oh, you're newly-weds!' my mother gushed, darting round the table to hug the couple like they were old friends instead of people she'd spotted for the first time five seconds ago. Billy Prosser squirmed, but Belinda looked quite pleased to be hugged.

'While we're waiting for our final guest,' Roderick said, 'let's go and meet our hosts in the library. Billy and Belinda have already met them,' he added as he led the rest of us back outside.

In the hall he knocked on another door.* A plummy voice on the other side shouted, 'Hello?'

Roderick looked in, said something, then turned back to us.

'In we go, people!'

---

* Well, no point knocking on the same door, was there?

He ushered the aged parents in, then us kids, who didn't want to go in at all. Why would we want to meet total strangers who called themselves 'Sir'? Bookcases stood floor-to-ceiling against three of the walls. The wall without a bookcase had pictures on it. The furniture was two lumpy couches and a desk, and that was it. A tweedy man with red cheeks and a big moustache and a woman with pale cheeks and no moustache sat on one of the couches. A younger couple sat on the other. The younger two didn't move, but the man with the moustache – Sir Duff Naffington – got up and showed his teeth, which were yellow. He held his hand out but didn't come any closer, which meant that those who felt they had to shake it (the Golden Oldies) had to go to him. It felt like being granted an audience with someone better than us, which I knew wouldn't go down well with Dad and Oliver.

The woman beside Sir Duff – his wife, Lady Helga – didn't get up, just lifted her arm to show us the back of her hand. The Oldies took turns holding it and dropping it. The young pair were the Naffingtons' daughter (Honor) and her boyfriend (Rudy Bollinger). No hands offered by them. Sir Duff looked a bit embarrassed about this. 'Quite the industrial magnate, young Rudy,' he said, like the news would lighten the atmosphere, which it didn't.

'We have one of those on the fridge,' said Oliver.

'Well, thank you, Sir Duff – indeed, all of you,' Roderick said. 'We'll leave you in peace now.'

Pete, Angie and I eyed one another. What a creep. Then we all backed out and Roderick closed the door super-quietly like he didn't want to disturb the prayers going on inside. Back in the hall he went to a little table and picked up a brass handbell, which he whirled over his head like someone whose sanity just flew out the window. The sound of the bell was so sudden and loud that every heel except Roderick's left the rug and every ear grew three times larger.

'Sir?'

A stiff geezer in black stood in a doorway that had been empty seconds before. He was one of those too-handsome-for-heaven types, very upright, with black, slicked-back hair and the kind of expression that gave you the idea that he didn't like the smell of his upper lip.

'Bogart,' said Roderick, 'be a good fellow and show our guests to their rooms, would you?'

The man gave a tiny little nod. 'This way, ladies and gentlemen – and young people.'

'Young people' was said with something too like a sneer for my liking.

'Bogart is Sir Duff's butler,' Roderick told us as

the stiff started up the ultra-wide staircase. 'He'll be looking after you while you're here.'

The word 'butler' ping-ponged silently back and forth between all of us except my mother, who must have known in advance that there was a butler here. Bogart was several stairs up before everyone else got it together and started after him. The staircase turned twice, sharply, before finally making it to the landing, which went round three of the walls. From up there you could look right down into the hall, not that Pete, Angie and I did. We didn't even want to *be* there. Bogart showed our parents to their rooms, which had wardrobes as big as beach huts and double beds with carved headboards ten centimetres thick. There were two other rooms as well as theirs. The door of one was open. A couple of suitcases lay on the bed.

'Mr and Mrs Prosser's room,' Bogart told us, like we'd asked. 'The other...' − he nodded at the closed door − '...is for Mr Tozer, when he *eventually* gets here. Shall I bring your luggage up?' he asked the dads.

'We can manage,' said Oliver. He hates the idea of servants. He doesn't even like being waited on in restaurants.

'Where do *we* go?' Angie asked Bogart the butler.

'You?' he said. 'You have the entire attic, all to yourselves.'

He pulled open a white door in an alcove you could easily miss. Steep narrow stairs with a manky old carpet climbed up from the other side of the door. It looked pretty gloomy at the top of the stairs.

'Better not jump around up there,' Bogart said. 'The floor's very old. Wouldn't want you tumbling into the rooms below, would we?' He gave a wicked smile as he turned away, like he would love to see us do just that.

We climbed the stairs, Angie in the lead, elbows drawn into her waist so her hands wouldn't be tempted to touch the walls. The higher we got the gloomier it became, but at the top there was a light switch. Angie flicked it. A couple of bare bulbs came on – slowly, like they could think of dozens of other things they would rather do. Facing the stairs was a half-open door. We looked in. A toilet. A toilet so ancient that its flusher was a piece of brown rope with knots in it. 'No,' Angie said. 'No, no, no.' We knew what that meant. Angie's been known to hold it in for hours rather than use toilets half as crappy as that one. She also wasn't tremendously happy that the only place to wash was a tiny sink next to the bog. She's quite big on washing, don't ask me why. I tell her that too much water on the skin will wrinkle it before it's ready, but she doesn't listen.

The ceiling of the attic sloped so steeply on one side

that if you didn't want to walk like an ape you had to stick to the other side of the room. Actually it was three rooms, but as they were separated by archways, not doors, it felt like one, with hiccups. Each room was a disaster area packed with the sort of junk that normal people chuck or burn.

'It's worse than your room at home,' I said to Pete.

'Which is really saying something,' said Ange.

Wherever you looked there were things to fall over, squeeze around or duck. There were bookcases stuffed with geriatric books, rickety bits of furniture including a desk with half a leg missing, piles of office files, tin buckets and spades like kids took to the beach in olden times, cardboard boxes, wooden boxes, plastic boxes, a baby's cot, and a whole lot more, including loads of prehistoric toys. Pete went to a clockwork train set on a big table. 'Bet this hasn't been played with since the middle of the last century,' he said, shunting a train along some rails.

'I bet no one's been *up* here since then,' I said.

There were four beds, singles, two in each of the end rooms. They looked like they'd been left unmade by the last people to sleep in them two generations ago. Angie was about as impressed with the state of the beds as she was with the toilet. I noticed a small green door tucked between the bookcases. 'Wonder what's through there?' I said.

'Woh, look at this!' said Pete as I started towards the green door.

'In a minute,' I said.

'No, not in a minute. Now!'

I cranked around. So did Angie. When we saw what had got Pete so agitated we just gaped. In a corner of the roof, covered with cobwebs and swinging ever so slightly because Pete had bumped into it, was a rope.

In the shape of a noose.

CHAPTER THREE

Once our hair had stopped standing on end and we'd reassembled our spines, we decided that the noose must have been left there as a joke by the last kids who were forced to sleep in the attic.

'Some joke,' said Pete. 'You want a joke? I can tell you a joke.'

'Don't bother,' said Angie.

'Why do scuba divers fall out of their boat backwards?'

'I said don't bother.'

'Because if they fell forwards they'd still be in the boat,' said Pete.

We went downstairs.

'I want a dialogue with my mother,' I said. 'She's the one who organised this weekend. She's the one who can think again.'

Dad and Oliver were struggling up the stairs with the carloads of bags and cases that no Golden Oldie female seems able to leave home without. We stepped aside to avoid getting smacked by passing luggage.

Audrey came out of her and Ollie's room and took a tiny bag off him. Swearing under his breath, he followed her in with the rest of their stuff. Pete and Angie followed him. I went after Dad.

'Dad,' I said, 'have people really been murdered here?'

'I'm out of breath,' he said breathlessly.

'Yeah, but have people really been murdered here?'

'Ask your mother.'

'She isn't here or I would. Where is she?'

'How would I know?' he snarled, flinging a suitcase onto the bed.

'What are you in a mood about?' I asked him.

He whirled on me. 'What am I in a mood about? What do you think I'm in a mood about? I'm in a mood about being here, where I don't want to be, when I should be at home indulging in my favourite Friday evening pastime, which is doing sweet sod all with my feet up.'

'You agreed to come,' I pointed out.

'You think I had a choice?' he said. 'You know your mother. Turns the house into a silent warzone if she doesn't get her way. Don't slam the door on your way out.'

I slammed the door on my way out.

'My dad's not happy,' I said to P & A when we regrouped.

27

'Nor's mine,' said Pete.

'My mum's quite excited,' said Angie.

'What about?' I asked her.

'Still wouldn't say.'

'You don't think they were committed up there, do you?' I said, nodding ceilingward.

'Think what were committed up there?'

'Murders. Where we'll be sleeping for two long nights.'

She bared her teeth at me, not in a smile. 'Thanks, McCue. That's the conclusion I was trying *not* to come to.'

'Can we get out of here?' said Pete.

'You mean make a break for it?' I said.

'I mean get out of the house.'

'Where to? We're miles from everywhere.'

'There's the garden.'

'You want to walk in a garden?' I said. 'You? Walk? In a garden?'

'It's all there is.'

As we went downstairs this fair-haired female person started up. She was about forty, I guessed, and she wore a little black dress and a white apron and a cap with lacy edges. She looked ridiculous. She stopped as we approached and bobbed her head. 'Hello,' she said. 'I'm Myrtle. You must be our weekend guests.'

We confessed that we were three of them. Angie asked if she lived there.

'I change the beds,' Myrtle said.

'Into what?' said Pete.

'And do the cleaning, polishing, serve the food. Me and Mona.'

'Mona?'

'The other maid.'

'Oh, you're a *maid*,' said Angie.

'Yes, miss.'

Angie mouthed, 'Miss?' at me, and Pete muttered, 'First a butler, now maids. Talk about how the other half lives.'

'Have people really been murdered here?' I asked Myrtle the maid. This looked like becoming my question of the day.

Myrtle giggled – 'Not yet!' – and ran upstairs much too girlishly for someone that old.

'Not *yet*?' said Angie, watching her go.

We carried on down and crossed the hall to the front door, which we opened. (We were new here, but opening the door seemed a fair way of getting to the other side of it.) Outside, a small yellow and red van with 'Haddenuff Catering' on the side had just pulled in behind the parked cars. We turned sharp left to avoid the people getting out of the van and scooted along the side of the house. We turned the corner at the end and walked some more, until —

'Hello, younguns! Exploring, are we?'

It was Roderick, trotting down some stone steps that curved up to a door into the house.

'Just mooching,' said Angie.

'Good, good. Lots to see, eh?'

'Spoilt for choice,' said Pete.

Rod the Bod jogged off and we ambled to the round tower built into another corner of the house. An old black drainpipe ran almost all the way down the side of the tower. The pipe ended at about head height because the last section had come away. The last section lay where it had fallen, quite a while ago judging by the weeds growing over it. We kicked the pipe (because it was there) and went on to the next corner, the final one, which we didn't turn because then we'd have been back where we started, and took off into the garden.

The garden looked like it had made itself up as it went along, then decided not to bother any more. It was really rambling, with stacks of big old trees, overgrown bushes, crumbling bits of wall, paths going nowhere, steps up and down to different levels. There were crumbly old statues standing in bushes like they were looking for their missing arms and noses, and an old greenhouse with dead plants inside, and vegetable patches without vegetables, and…well, you get the idea.

We hadn't quite seen all of these stunning sights when Pete pulled his phone out and started jabbing keys. I asked who he was texting.

'The world,' he said. 'I want it to know what a rubbish place this is.'

'Oh, look,' said Angie suddenly. 'A secret garden door!'

The door was in a crumbly old wall with green stuff hanging over the top. The door was dark blue. Looked like it had been painted a couple of wars ago.

'You don't know there's a garden the other side of it,' I said.

'Has to be, door like that.'

'No signal,' said Pete.

'What?' I said.

He held his phone up. 'Zip.'

'Maybe you have to be higher up.' I indicated the big old tree we stood by.

'Maybe you do.'

He started up the tree.

'You're not ten any more,' Angie said to his backside.

'You don't have to be ten to climb trees,' I said, tempted to shin up after him. It'd been a while since I'd climbed a good tree.

'Oi, geddown from there!'

Angie and I whirled round. A man stood about ten metres away, beside an empty wheelbarrow.

'I'm trying to get a signal,' Pete said from the tree.

'Down! Now!'

Pete cursed, but dropped down.

'Where did you spring from?' Angie asked the man.

'I'll tell ee where I sprung from, young madam,' he growled in this catch-all country yokel accent. 'I sprung from this garrden 'ere and oi be lookin' out fer what's in it, and one thing the boss don't like is kids climbin' 'is trees, so don't you do it please, and I don't care oo you be.'

'Sorry, he didn't know,' Angie said. 'I'll chain him up from now on. I'm Angie, and you are…?'

'Silas Blackthorrn,' the man said. '*Misterr* Blackthorrn to you.'

He was a funny looking geezer, with a big red nose and a heavy scowl, and a lop-sided stoop like he had an invisible sack of bricks on one shoulder. He wore a check cap with strands of hair hanging from inside it like they came with it, and an old tweed jacket with leather elbow patches, and he had this bushy brown beard that looked like it had been stuck on in a hurry rather than grown over time.

'You're the gardener then, are you?' Angie asked Mr Blackthorn.

'That oi be,' said he, gripping the handles of his empty wheelbarrow. 'There be three of us as a rule, the two lads an' me, but they got their 'oliday time, which ain't convenient at all, not at all.'

He pushed his barrow past us, towards the secret garden door.

'Nice to meet you, Mr Blackthorn!' Angie said to his back.

I couldn't swear to it, but it sounded like Mr B said, 'Wish oi could say the same,' as he kicked the door open and shoved his wheelbarrow through.

'I can't believe you said that,' I said to Angie as the door slammed. '"You're the gardener then, are you?" He couldn't have been more like a gardener if he'd done three years at Gardener Stereotype University.'

'I was just making conversation,' she said. 'Someone had to.'

'No, they didn't. They really didn't.'

We were in no hurry to go back to the house and all that servant-master stuff, or our lousy attic with the swinging noose, so we carried on mooching. We came to a small pond half covered with lily pads, and had stopped to look at it with total boredom when something fell out of a tree onto Angie's shoulder and bounced off. She squealed. The something was a frog. A big brown one. It gazed up at us from the ground like we were invading its patch, and hopped away. Angie fluttered a hand over her heart.

'Why me? Why *me*?'

'You're a girl,' said Pete.

She glared at him. 'So?'

'Frogs prefer girls. Well-known fact.'

'I've never heard it before.'

'No, me neither.'

When we came upon a little potting shed with a half-open door, we peered in, like you do with open doors. All the usual gardeny stuff inside – flowerpots, cobwebs, watering cans, rakes, cobwebs, spades, ancient garden shears with the pointy end bits broken off, cobwebs, bags of this, packets of that, cobwebs...

'Why are we looking in here?' said Pete.

We moved on, and a minute later came to a small clearing surrounded by bushes. In the clearing there was a tall flat stone at the head of two mounds of earth. There were words on the stone.

KEITH AND SYLVIA
CUT DOWN
IN THEIR PRIME
MUCH MOURNED

'Parents of the owner?' Angie wondered.

'People don't bury their parents in the garden,' I said.

'They might if they had one this big,' said Pete, fiddling with his phone again.

'Maybe they were murdered,' said Angie.

'Why would they have been murdered?' I said.

'"Come and meet Roderick and hear about the murders," your mum said. Maybe it's these murders he wants to tell us about.'

'Still no signal,' said Pete. 'Place is like a dead zone.'

I looked at Angie. Angie looked at me. Dead zone? We're standing over a pair of graves in a garden and he says it's like a *dead* zone?

Just then we heard a sound from the house.

'A dinner gong?' said Angie.

'It's that sort of place,' I said.

'That butler might not let us near the table if we're late,' said Pete.

'If the food's as old as everything else here, I might not mind,' said Ange.

We started back anyway.

On the way, I thought, Dead zone.

Then I thought it again.

Dead zone.

And again.

35

Dead zone.

And I thought about nooses and murders and graves in the garden, and I shivered.

What *was* all this?

CHAPTER FOUR

The red and yellow van wasn't in the courtyard any more, but just as we got to the front door a sports car zoomed up the drive and parked alongside our two. The man who got out waved at us, but we didn't know him so we put our heads down and shot inside.

'Where've you been?' my dad asked.

He and Oliver were just standing there, like spares. Across the room Lady Helga Naffington was playing some Oldie tune on the piano. I was surprised. She looked like the snooty old-dear type who wouldn't be seen stuffed in the same part of her house as commoners like us.

'Checking out the garden,' I said to Dad.

'No one knew where you were. We tried to phone you, no signal.'

'Yeah, we found that when we tried to call you to give our exact location every step and second of the way. What did you want?'

'Dinner's about to be served.'

'Ah, the magic words!' said a voice behind us

– sports-car man, who'd followed us in. He was all twinkly-eyed and smiley, and wore a check jacket and a brown trilby hat. He marched forward, hand outstretched. 'Tozer! Gerald!'

Oliver shook the hand because he was nearest to it. 'Garrett. Oliver.'

Then Dad took a turn. 'McCue. Mel.'

'And these are the offspring, no doubt!' the man said, whirling on the three of us so fast that we jumped back as one.

'Yeah, that's them,' said my dad. He didn't bother to give our names, in any order.

'Hello!' This was Audrey. She was sitting in one of the high-backed armchairs flicking through that old book, *Latin Names of Common Flowers*.

'Hi!' Gerald Tozer leaped at her as she got up. He pumped her hand like he wanted water to shoot out of her armpit.

Lady Helga carried on playing the piano like she was the only person for miles around.

'Ah, Mr Tozer, I presume. Just in time for *dinner*.'

Bogart the butler, suddenly there from nowhere, eyed the new arrival without a smudge of pleasure.

Mr T spun towards him. 'Hi there!'

He put the old hand out for another good shaking, but Bogart looked at it like it had just come out of a bucket of horse manure, and didn't shake it.

'If you wouldn't mind being shown to your room later,' he said coldly, 'you might like to accompany these *earlier* guests to the dining room.'

Mr Tozer looked like he'd been scolded, but I thought that put-down was quite cool. There were kids at school that I would love to pull stuff like that on. A couple of teachers too.

Lady Helga wasn't one of his followers when Bogart led the way to the dining room, but her piano playing stopped seconds after the door was closed.

The dining room table now had a heavy white cloth on it and places laid for us guests. The couple who'd been there last time we looked in – Belinda and Billy Prosser, the newly-weds – were still there, still sitting in one another's pockets. Pete threw himself into a chair the other side of the table from them.

'Not there!' said Bogart sharply.

'Why not?' said Pete.

'Because each place is designated.'

Bogart pointed at a little card between the knives and forks in front of Pete. The card had a name on it. Audrey Mint. All the other places had cards too, with different names.

'You three are over there,' Bogart said.

We trooped round the table and looked at our name

cards. Angie had been placed between me and Pete, which put Belinda Prosser on Pete's other side. I was at the end. There was a setting at the other end and four more across from us. Mr Tozer had been put next to my dad. Audrey Mint sat between Dad and Oliver. No sign of my mother.

We'd all just parked ourselves in the right seats when Roderick Basket-Case came in, beaming.

'All here now, I see. Great. After dinner I'll tell you everything you need to know, but for now let's peruse the menu and choose our fare.'

He sat down, at the head of the table, which left nowhere for Mum when she eventually joined us. Someone needs to rethink the seating arrangements, I thought as we all picked up the little menu cards in front of us.

RODERICK'S MURDER MENU

A MANIAC'S CHOICE OF DEATHLY DELICACIES

SCREAMING STARTER
Carotid artery and coriander soup
Smoked-to-last-gasp mackerel pâté
Nastily skewered kebab
(served with guillotined French sticks)

MURDEROUS MAIN COURSE
Strangled chicken
Gutted salmon with death's-head dill
Suffocated vegetarian lasagne
(served with cruelly sliced vegetables)

POISONED PUDDING
Chocolate Torture (torte)
Frozen-to-death icecream
Bloodberry cheesecake

I noticed Roderick watching us with a big grin and leaned towards Angie's nearest ear. 'Is he sick or something?' I whispered.

'The signs are not good,' she whispered back.

'There's nothing with chips,' said Pete.

'You can't have chips all the time,' I said round Ange.

'I don't see why not,' he said.

'Where's your mum?' Angie asked me.

'No idea. Or where she's going to sit.'

'Maybe she's run out on us.'

'What, gone home and left us here?'

'Who knows?'

'Dad's still here. So are Aud and Ollie. She wouldn't have left them too – would she?'

She shrugged. 'Something weird's going on, and I don't like it.'

'Whatever it is,' I said, 'it has to be better than being sent away to boarding school, like you thought.'

I went back to my menu.

'Jig...' Angie said after a pause.

'What?'

'Your mum.'

I looked up. 'What about her?'

She nodded towards two women who'd come in. One of them was Myrtle from the stairs. The other was my mother. And Myrtle wasn't the only one dressed as a maid now. I gaped as the two of them started going round asking what everyone wanted to eat and writing the orders on little pads.

'Your mother's *working* here?' said Pete, almost as dazed as me.

'As a *maid*?' said Angie.

'But she's *got* a job!' I said. 'Near where we live.'

'Perhaps she lost it and took this instead,' said Pete.

'No, that'd be crazy, even for her. She couldn't commute all this way twice a day.'

'Wouldn't have to if it's a live-in job,' said Ange.

I stared at her. 'You mean live here, not at home?'

'I dunno. Have to ask her.'

'I would, but she's not taking orders on this side.'

'Any chips?' Pete asked Myrtle, who'd just got to him. There weren't.

42

My mother glanced at me as she went round the table, but looked away quickly when I gave her a 'What the hell?' stare.

'While we're waiting for our food,' Roderick said when Mum and Myrtle had taken the orders and left, 'allow me to tell you a bit about the house. Naffington Hall was built around 1820 by Emanuel Naffington, a businessman with connections, on the site of a monastery that had fallen into disrepair following Henry VIII's purges...'

That was just the beginning. Once he'd milked the history of the place he moved on to the architecture, every little feature of it, even bits that were so tucked away no one ever saw them. He yammered on through the starters and most of the main course. I could tell from looking at Dad and Oliver that I wasn't the only one who wished he'd shut his trap and let us chew our chow in peace.

We were halfway through what the menu called 'pudding' when Billy Prosser said, 'Excuse me, got to phone the office,' and stood up.

'But, Billy, it's our weekend,' his new wife said in a whiny little voice.

'I know, darling,' he said, 'but they're expecting me to call in at this time. There's that big deal going down, remember? Shan't be long. Forgive me, everyone.'

He dabbed his lips with a napkin, dropped it on his chair and left the room. Belinda looked like he'd walked out on her for good, and the room went quiet till Roderick said something unfunny and Gerald Tozer chuckled like chuckling was his job. We went back to stuffing our faces, but I couldn't concentrate on food. Couldn't get it out of my head that my mother was suddenly doing maidy type stuff at this place.

I leaned towards Angie's ear once more. 'Any idea where the kitchen is?'

'Why?'

'I need words with my female parent.'

'No idea, but it can't be far.'

I pushed my chair back.

'Where you going?' Dad asked.

'Forgot something,' I said.

'What?'

'I forget.'

I left the room. Out in the hall I looked for signs of a kitchen. There was a corridor off to the right, with some doors in it. The nearest door was half open. I went to it and looked round it. A desk, an armchair, a couple of filing cabinets. Not a kitchen. I heard the clatter of crockery from the next door along. I went to it. Looked in. Saw Myrtle, who saw me.

'Hello,' she said. 'You lost?'

'I'm looking for my mother.'

'Your mother?'

'The other one who took orders at the table and brought the food.'

'Oh, Mona.'

'Mona? No, her name's not...'

A door at the back of the room opened and my mother came in. She jerked to a halt when she saw me, and looked instantly guilty.

'You,' I said. 'We have things to discuss.'

She opened her mouth, but before words could leap out of it, there was a sharp bang from somewhere behind me.

Myrtle jumped. 'What was that?'

'Sounded like a balloon bursting,' I said.

I looked back the way I'd come and, sure enough, saw a burst balloon (a blue one) on the floor some way along. But there was something else too – some*one* – lying in the hall, not moving.

'He wasn't there just now,' I said.

'Who wasn't?' my maidish mother asked from the kitchen.

'I'm the one with questions for *you*,' I said. 'Stay right there!'

I started back along the corridor, wanting to check out the person on the floor. Someone beat me to the

45

scene, though: Roderick, flinging the dining room door back and gasping when he saw who was lying there.

'Sir Duff!'

It was Sir Duff all right. He lay on his front, head on one side, eyes shut. Rod's eyes flipped from Sir Duff to me.

'What happened?'

I shrugged. 'I was along there. All I heard was a balloon.'

'Balloon?'

I nodded at the flat blue balloon, but he seemed more interested in Sir Duff. He sank to one knee and felt his neck (Sir D's, not his own).

'He's dead,' he said.

'He's what?' I said.

'Dead,' he said.

'Dead?' I said.

'Yes,' he said. 'And...'

'And?' I said.

'From the look of that hole in his temple...'

'Hole in his temple?'

'And with no sign of a gun,'

'No sign of a gun?' I said.

'It looks like he's been...'

'Been what?' I said.

'Murdered!' he said.

CHAPTER FIVE

I'd never seen a murdered corpse before, so you might not be surprised to hear that my jaw was still somewhere around my lower ribcage when everyone streamed out of the dining room to see what was up.

'Woh!' said Pete, spotting the body.

'What's he doing on the floor?' said Angie.

'Not a huge amount,' I said, ramming my jaw back in place. 'He' – meaning Roderick – 'says that he' – meaning Sir Duff – 'has been whacked.'

'Whacked?'

'Murdered. To death.'

'Woh,' said Pete.

'I thought it was a balloon bursting,' I said.

'Balloon?' said Ange.

'That one.'

I nodded at the burst balloon on the floor. Angie looked towards it.

'I see no balloon.'

Nor could I. It wasn't there any more. The burst balloon had flown.

'Can we be sure he's dead?' one of the adults said.

'Sure, if we had a gun to shoot him again,' said Oliver.

'Shut up, Ollie,' said Audrey.

'But who could have done such a thing?' said Belinda Prosser in this tiny little-girl voice that you felt should have had a lisp.

'Maybe we should ask your husband,' Gerald Tozer said to her.

'My husband? Billy went to ring his firm. You saw him leave.'

'Yes. Exactly. He wasn't in the room when the gun went off.'

'Nor was Jiggy,' said Pete.

'Thanks, Pete,' I said.

'What's that in his hand?' said Audrey.

She meant Sir Duff's. Roderick started to open it.

'Should you be touching him?' asked Gerald Tozer.

'Probably not,' Roderick said, but he finished opening it anyway.

In the hand lay a bunch of these little white flowers with red stalks. We might have wondered why a dead person would be holding flowers, but just then Lady Helga ran out of another room and fell to her knees beside her husband's body.

'Duff! Oh, Duff!'

Her daughter wasn't a million miles behind her. Her boyfriend, Rudy Bollinger, sauntered onto the scene from somewhere else. Rudy looked kind of amused. Honor didn't. She joined her mother on her knees beside the body. Pete, Angie and I just stood there, on the edge of things. I didn't know what to say or do or think, and they looked like they were having the same problem. I saw Billy Prosser step out of a side room, then Myrtle and my mother coming along the corridor from the kitchen. When Myrtle saw Sir Duff she gave an ear-shrivelling shriek, then another shriek, and once she'd got the hang of it she went on shrieking shriek after shriek after shriek.

'Bogart!' Roderick shouted. 'Calm that maid!'

I don't know where Bogart came from, but as he started towards Myrtle, my mother said, 'It's all right, I'll see to her,' and hustled Myrtle away. Once they were out of sight, Myrtle stopped shrieking.

'I'd better call the police,' said Bogart.

He went to this old-style phone on a little table near the front door. While he was on the blower, Roderick got up to give Lady Helga and her daughter more room to sob over Sir Duff's body. Rudy Bollinger stood gazing down at it with his hands in his pockets like this was something that happened every day.

'I think that now would be a fine time for a little

chat,' Roderick said. 'Guests – to the library, if you please!'

All of us guests trooped into the library. The Naffington females, Rudy Bollinger and Bogart stayed in the hall. So did Sir Duff.

'Pray be seated,' Roderick said, closing the door behind us.

He was smiling. He found this funny? I glanced at Pete and Angie. They didn't find it funny. Nor did I. We were still trying to get over seeing a dead body. A dead *murdered* body.

Roderick went to the mantelpiece and leaned against it while the six adult guests packed themselves onto the two couches and us kids sat on the floor because there was nowhere else. Roderick couldn't have looked more relaxed if he'd just had an hour's head massage.

'Now as some of you know, all is not quite as it seems here,' he began. 'The house is indeed called Naffington Hall, but no Naffingtons have lived here for over seventy years. It's owned by a friend of mine who, for a small fee, has agreed to let me use it for my little business venture.'

Pete, Angie and I looked at one another. No Naffingtons? Then who...?

'Of course, no money will change hands this weekend,' Roderick went on. 'This is a trial run, to see if we've got it right and to test the reactions of you, our special guests, but subsequent guests will be expected to shell out for our...' He chuckled. '...services.'

Again, the three of us looked at each other. *Services?*

Roderick pushed himself away from the mantelpiece and strode to one of the bookcases. A large board stood against the shelves, facing away from us. He turned the board round for us to read.

THE PURE ISLE PLAYERS PRESENT...

MURDER WEEKENDS AT NAFFINGTON HALL

Dinner, breakfast, mayhem and murder.
Residents are being cruelly killed.
Who by?
And why?
Can you solve these dastardly crimes?
Prices (and murders) on application.

Yet again, the three of us looked at the others of us. We were getting fed up of looking at one another, but there was no one else of kid age.

'Murder weekends?' I said.

'Dastardly crimes?' said Pete.

'Prices on application?' said Angie.

Roderick's lips twitched. 'The youngsters haven't been informed of the true nature of things, I believe. Well,' he said, 'you're here to sample my theatre troupe's first excursion into murder mystery programming. With public interest in the theatre currently in something of a slump, I'm hoping a sideline like this will keep us in the black.'

'Theatre troupe?' I said. 'Not the one my mum's in?'

'The very same. We are The Pure Isle Players,' he added proudly.

'Pure Isle Players?' said my dad.

'Yes.'

Dad chuckled. 'Funnily enough, she's never mentioned the name of her am-dram mob. Pure Isle, eh? Anything to do with the quality of the acting?'

Roderick gave him a tight little smile. 'It's where I was born.'

'What is?'

'Pure Isle.'

'Never heard of it.'

'Not many have. But you've heard of Fair Isle?'

'I had a Fair Isle sweater once when I was young.' This was Oliver.

Roderick turned to him. 'Made with Fair Isle wool, of course. Pure Isle lies very near Fair Isle. It's often referred to as Fair Isle's baby sister.'

'So while Fair Isle's famous for wool,' Oliver said, 'Pure Isle's famous for people leaving and starting theatre groups?'

'I prefer the word "troupe",' Roderick said.

'My mum's not got a job here as a maid then,' I said. 'She's playing a part.'

'Indeed she is. As is everyone else apart from you guests. And me, of course.'

'The butler and Myrtle?' said Angie.

'And Sir Duff, Lady Helga, Honor, Rudy Bollinger. Pure Isle Players all.'

'So it *was* a balloon,' I said. 'A balloon and a fake hole in the head.' But then I had a thought. 'Hang on. I was the first to see Sir Duff's body. I really thought he was dead. If I had a weak bladder, I might have wet myself.'

He guffawed heartily. 'Good to know we had you fooled! What you all have to do between now and Sunday lunchtime is decide who did the foul deed. And to help you keep track of events...'

From a desk drawer he took a batch of little notepads and pens. He walked among us, handing them out.

'Keep these with you at all times. When you see or hear something that might have some relevance, or which you think might be a clue, jot it down.'

As he finished handing out the pads and pens there was a mighty clanging sound. The front doorbell.

'That'll be the rozzers!' he said, rubbing his hands.

He shot out. The adults got to their feet and went after him. Even Dad and Oliver got up, though not as eagerly as the Prossers, Mr Tozer and Audrey.

'And you two knew about this, did you?' I said to the dads accusingly.

'We would've told you,' Ollie said. 'But we had instructions to keep shtoom on pain of a Weight Watchers diet.'

'A clue would've been nice,' said Pete.

'Clues are what this rubbish is all about,' said Dad. 'Clues, murder, blood. Pretty sick if you ask me. Your mother and her daft ideas.'

'I'll murder her when I see her,' I said.

'And I won't testify against you.' He sighed. 'Well, I suppose we'll have to go along with it and chat to the phoney coppers.'

'The police are actors too then,' said Angie.

'If they're not,' said Oliver, 'we could all be chucked in the dungeons for wasting police time.'

We went out to the hall. Bogart the phoney butler was over by the front door talking to a man in a raincoat.

'Only one cop?' I said.

'Maybe they ran out of actors,' said Pete.

'Hey, the body's gone,' said Angie.

She was right. Sir Duff was no longer on the floor. In his place was a white chalk outline showing where he'd been.

'Pretty nippy on his feet for a dead person,' said Pete.

'He probably had another part to play,' I said.

'And I think I can guess which,' said Angie, nodding towards the policeman.

'We're understaffed,' the copper was saying to Bogart, 'so I'm having to conduct this investigation solo.'

Bogart turned to us. 'Ladies and gentlemen, allow me to introduce Inspector Qwerty.'

'Good evening, Inspector,' sang a couple of the guests.

'Evening,' the fake inspector grunted. 'I'll be wanting to know where you all were at the time of the murder, and will interview you shortly, one by one.'

'It's him all right,' Pete whispered.

I agreed. Sir Duff Naffington had had a big moustache and the policeman didn't. Sir Duff had been round-shouldered and a bit paunchy and the policeman was very upright and on the thin side. They also spoke in different accents and voices. But there was still a likeness. Part of the likeness was the smudge of red on the inspector's temple.

'So he's investigating his own death,' Angie said.

'He might as well, cos I'm not playing,' growled Pete.

'They seem keen enough,' I said. Four of the guests had gathered round the inspector like they wanted his autograph.

'Unlike the dads,' said Ange.

Ollie and my father looked like they'd been condemned to a weekend partying with five-year-olds and couldn't wait for it to be over. I noticed someone peeking round the dining room door. My mother, the maid.

'Oi, Mona,' I said. 'Stay where you are! I want words with you!'

I stormed towards her.

CHAPTER SIX

'This can go, right away,' said Pete, yanking down the noose in our poxy old attic.

If he hadn't torn it down I would have, because it was obvious now that the noose had been hung there to make us nervous, and we weren't happy about it. Any of it. Murder weekend? How gross. And how insulting not to have been told about it before we got there. Parents. They have no respect for their kids.

The only non-electric light in the attic came from four little windows, and we were so high up that all we could see through them was tree tops. There was only one door apart from the ones at the foot of the stairs and on the toilet – the little green door between the bookcases. It looked like a cupboard door, so when Pete opened it to chuck the noose in we were surprised to see daylight. Well, evening light. Pete said, 'Hey,' and we followed him out onto a flat grey roof about five metres square. Other roofs, tiled ones, sloped up from ours on three sides. The fourth side – the corner of the house – was occupied by the tall round tower that we'd seen from outside. In the side of the tower there was a door with an iron handle. Pete twisted and tugged the handle, but the door wouldn't budge.

Battlements lined the edge of our bit of roof. We leaned out between them. Way below we could see the lily pond where the frog had jumped onto Angie's shoulder. Also the potting shed. There was someone in the shed doorway. The miserable gardener we'd met earlier.

'I wonder if he's another of the actors?' said Angie.

'He's the gardener,' I said.

'He could be playing the part. You said it yourself, he's a total cliché. He couldn't be more like a stereotypical gardener if he tried.'

'Let's see how he likes this cliché,' said Pete.

He lobbed the noose. It didn't hit the gardener, but it landed near enough to make him jump. We pulled back in a hurry, laughing for the first time since we'd arrived at Naff Hall.

Back in the attic, we started rooting through stuff to see if there was anything interesting enough to distract us from this rubbish weekend. Pete's big find – a box of marbles – so excited him that he almost fell asleep standing up.

'Can anyone tell me what marbles are for?' he asked, rolling some across the floor.

'They're for what you're doing now,' I said.

'I'm just rolling them across the floor.'

'Well, congratulations, you've cracked it.'

He put the marbles back in the box.

Our beds were still in the state they'd been in when we first saw them. 'You'd think the maids would have changed them,' Angie said.

'They might have if they were real maids,' I said.

She sat down on the one she'd chosen for herself at the opposite end to the ones she'd said were Pete's and mine. 'Your mother should be made to pay for doing this to us, Jig,' she said.

'She will. I'm not loading the dishwasher for a month when we get home.'

'What did she say when you confronted her?'

'She said she'd wanted it to be a surprise.'

'Well, she got that right. And that was it?'

'Just about. When I started in on her she went all downcast, the way she does when she's criticised. I always feel bad when she does that, even when I've done nothing.'

'I suppose her motives were good,' Angie said generously.

'Good how? Solving a murder to relieve exam stress.'

I whipped out Roderick's pen and notepad. 'We

have the technology to do *that*!' I said, pasting a big fake grin on my handsome features.

She glared at me, then chucked her own pen and pad under the bed. So did Pete. I shoved mine back in my pocket before they could snatch them off me. The pen wasn't bad for a freebie.

'Do we have to stay in all weekend?' Pete said.

'There's nowhere to go apart from the garden, and we've done that,' Angie said.

'I saw a signpost to a village as we turned into the drive,' I said.

'A village out here,' she said, 'is probably just two cottages and a dog.'

'There might be more,' I said, shooting for optimism.

'Yeah. A sweet shop, a vandalised phone box, maybe a broken-down tractor if we're really on a roll.'

Pete brightened. 'Sweet shop?'

'Angie! Pete! Jiggy! May I come up?'

Audrey's voice, from the foot of our stairs.

'If you *must*,' Angie said tetchily.

Her mother's feet on the stairs. 'So this is where you've been put,' she said when she made it to the top.

'Imprisoned,' said Angie. 'I'll never forgive you for going along with this.'

'It's only for the weekend,' said Audrey.

'A *long* weekend. A *very* long weekend.'

'Oh, it's going to be fun, you'll see. We're all wanted in the library. The inspector's going to question us about our whereabouts when the murder was committed.'

'You can tell him our whereabouts,' Angie said. 'We were in the dining room, with you. Well, Pete and I were.'

'Would you rather sit up here than tell him yourselves?' Audrey asked.

'Up here?' said Ange. 'You jest, Mother.'

We followed her down to the library. The other guests were there, plus the inspector, still in his raincoat. No sign of Roderick. No loss.

'Ah, the youngsters!' the inspector said as we went in.

'Ah, the phoney copper,' muttered Pete.

The inspector closed the door and kicked off the Q&As by asking us all, as a group, what we'd been doing at the time of the murder.

'Stuffing our faces,' Oliver grunted.

'Without chips,' said Pete.

'All of you?'

'He left,' Angie said, pointing at Billy Prosser.

'I've explained that,' said Billy. 'I had to make a business call.'

'A likely story,' I said.

'It can't be him,' said Pete. 'He's not one of the cast.'

61

The inspector looked puzzled. 'Cast? I don't understand.'

Pete sighed. 'No, course you don't. OK, it was him, he was the murderer, can we go now?' He reached for the door handle.

'Stop!' the inspector said sharply.

Pete froze. The inspector glared around the room.

'This is a murder investigation, and until I clear you of any involvement, I'd be obliged if you would all answer my questions in a civilised and sensible fashion.'

'It's the staff you ought to be talking to, not us,' said Gerald Tozer.

The inspector turned to him. 'Thank you for explaining my job to me, sir. And you are?'

'Gerald Tozer.'

The inspector frowned. 'Tozer?'

'Yes. Why do you say it like that?'

'It's an unusual name, that's all.'

Gerald did not look pleased. 'Yes, well, Qwerty isn't exactly common either, *Inspector.*'

There were more questions – pointless ones, because the whole scenario must have been worked out in advance by Roderick and his mob, who knew who the 'murderer' was and would either be dropping hints or trying to steer us away from working it out too soon. The three of us and Dad and Ollie did a fair bit of eyebrow raising at one another, but Audrey and the Prossers soon got into it – Gerald Tozer too, after a while. When the inspector told us he'd got all he needed from us for the moment and that he would now 'quiz the household staff' we left the library. 'Grand stuff, eh?' Gerald said as we went.

'Load of cobblers,' said my dad.

'Not your sort of thing, old chap?' Gerald asked.

'It'd be more like it if I could drink myself into oblivion,' Dad said.

'The butler should know where there's some booze,' said Billy Prosser.

'He's just an actor playing a part,' said Oliver.

'Yes, the part of the butler. It's his role to serve drinks.'

'Worth testing,' said Dad. He snatched the handbell from the little table and whirled it round his head, deafening all of us.

'Gentlemen?'

Bogart had slithered out of the woodwork, all stiff-backed and superior.

'Any chance of something to take the edge off?' Dad asked him.

'Edge off, sir?'

'Being here. Something alcoholic.'

Bogart looked down his nose at his top lip and said that he would see if he could track down a bottle of wine.

'We don't want wine, we want beer,' said Oliver.

'There's no *beer* on the premises, sir,' Bogart said. He said 'beer' like other people might say 'dead rats'.

'Scotch then,' said Ollie.

Bogart sniffed. 'Her Ladyship rather frowns on strong alcohol, but I'll see what there is...sir.'

'What are we supposed to do while you lot drink yourselves under the rug?' Pete asked as Bogart merged with the woodwork again.

Gerald nodded at a door we hadn't seen the other side of yet. 'Games room, if it's of interest. Poked my head in while having a nose after the murder.'

'Might as well take a look,' said Pete.

The games room wasn't huge and there wasn't a lot in it, just a pool table, a ping-pong table, a couple of card tables, a dart board. A book lay on the pool table: *Latin Names of Common Flowers*. We ping-ponged a bit, chucked some darts, shot some pool, and were soon bored out of our brains, so when Angie looked behind a curtain and discovered an unlocked door and some stone steps inside a circular wall, we thought we might as well see where they went.

'I think it's the tower,' she said as we climbed up

and up, round and round.

There were no lights on the way up, but every so often there was a tiny window. It was getting dark out, but there was enough light for us to see the steps, just about. Finally, breathing hard, we came to a door with an iron bolt. A very old iron bolt. The old iron bolt took some waggling, but we drew it back, the door swung out with a creak like a dirty old laugh and we were looking at the bit of grey roof outside our attic.

'So we could get in from here if we wanted,' said Angie.

'I don't want,' said Pete.

None of us did. We closed the door and carried on up the winding stairs. Round and round and round again, and in another minute we reached a little ladder leading to a trap door in the ceiling. Pete scooted up the ladder, forced the door's bolt back, let it fall and climbed onto the roof. Ange and I followed. The roof was about three metres across and circled by battlements. We were so high up now that we could see for miles, even though it was nearly dark. It felt like the top of the world up there. The view was of fields and trees and trees and fields and nothing much else in all directions.

Angie pointed a toe at a newish cigarette packet on the floor. 'Someone's been up here,' she said.

'Probably a no-smoking rule indoors,' said Pete.

'Bit of a climb for a gasper.'

'Yeah, but—'

'Listen,' I said.

'What to?' said Angie.

'I heard something. Voices. Male and female.'

They listened. We all did.

'Seems to be coming from there,' said Pete, meaning a little drain in the floor.

'It must drain into the pipe that runs down the side of the tower,' said Angie.

'What pipe?'

'The one with the last section missing – don't you remember? People must be standing close to the open end, and their voices are carrying all the way up to here.'

We squatted over the drain to get a better earful.

'You hated him,' one of the drained voices said. *'You made no secret of it, and you knew Mummy and I would get everything if he died, but to propose to me tonight – this night of all nights – how insensitive!'*

'Honor Naffington,' Angie whispered.

'But, darling, I've often mentioned marriage,' the male voice said – to Honor, not Angie. *'I'm only bringing it up again now because I thought that a firm proposal would be some consolation in your time of trial.'*

'That smarmy Bollinger character,' said Pete.

I de-squatted. Went to the battlements. Looked over the side. It was darker way down on the ground, but the light from the games room window which we'd left on fell on the two figures standing close together by the wall.

'*Oh, yes, marry me and you'll have access to everything,*' Honor said to Rudy and the drainpipe. '*As if I haven't given you enough to cover your gambling debts.*'

'*Honor, darling, you misjudge me,*' protested Rudy.

'They can't still be in character,' whispered Pete. 'There's no one about, so who would they be doing this for?'

'Us?' I said, turning from the battlements.

'Us? They don't know we're up here.'

'We *think* they don't.'

'How can they? There's a whole drainpipe between us and them.'

'Will you two shut up?' Angie hissed. 'I want to hear them, not you.'

We shut up and listened.

'*What I'd like to know,*' Honor said, '*is where you were when Daddy was shot.*'

'*Me? I was with you.*'

'*You weren't. You slipped out a minute after he did and we didn't see you again until after the shot was fired.*'

'I went for a smoke. House rule, no smoking indoors, remember?'

'Told you,' said Pete.

'How convenient!' said Honor. 'You're with us for an hour or more and the moment Daddy goes to check his diary you also make your excuses, and next thing we know he's been killed.'

'And you think I would do such a thing?' said Rudy.

'I'd prefer to think that you wouldn't. But I'm sure Inspector Qwerty will be fascinated to hear of the timing.'

'And when he comes back in the morning you'll tell him, will you?'

'If I don't, Mummy's sure to.'

'Oh, I wouldn't count on that. Your mother's quite fond of me.'

'Yes, you've rather won her over with your devilish charm.'

'I think I'd best say goodnight before this gets even more out of hand,' said Rudy. 'Perhaps you'll have a cooler head in the morning.'

'No, wait, Rudy, let's talk this through.'

'We've talked quite enough for one night, my sweet. Till tomorrow!'

And he obviously went because nothing more was said – until Honor's voice reached us once more.

She sounded startled.

'What are you doing here? Eavesdropping?'

Pete and Angie, still crowding the drain, sat back sharply.

'How did she know we were listening?' Angie whispered.

But Honor didn't mean us. I looked down from the battlements again. Someone else was talking to her now. A man in a hat. The man said something, but so quietly that we couldn't catch it or make out whose voice it was. Honor's reply was clear enough, though.

'You men. You're all the same. All you want is my money. Leave me alone! Leave me alone!'

Then she was running along the side of the house. The man in the hat didn't move for a few seconds. Then he turned and walked away in the opposite direction.

CHAPTER SEVEN

'I slept surprisingly well, considering,' Angie said, drifting in from her pit at the other end of the attic and kicking me awake.

'I'm so glad to hear that,' I said. 'But kick me one more time and you're over the battlements.'

She woke Pete with a chucked cushion. Three chucked cushions actually. He snored through the first two. That snoring had kept me awake half the night.

When we'd got ourselves together and popped some clothes on we trudged down to the dining room. We were up early for a Saturday, but not early enough for Bogart the phoney butler, who stood to attention outside the dining room like something out of a Stuffed Butler Museum.

'Breakfast is eight to nine-thirty,' he said, looking down his nose at us like he was trying to focus on a bogey on the end.

Pete glanced at his watch. 'It's nine-thirty-two.'

'Quite,' said Bogart. 'Two minutes past end of breakfast.'

'So we don't get fed?'

'Hmm! Well, I daresay that on this one occasion — this *sole* occasion — I might see if there's anything left.'

'Terrific,' said Pete.

As Bogart headed for the kitchen I wondered what parts he played at other times. He made a pretty good snooty butler, that's for sure.

'Morning, lads and ladette!' a voice rang out as we threw back the door of the dining room. Mr Tozer — Gerald — getting up from the table, where he'd been sitting with Dad, Ollie and Audrey.

'Who's he calling a ladette?' Angie said.

'All set to solve Sir Duff's murder?' Gerald asked, coming towards us. 'Can't beat a good old-fashioned murder, can you?'

'Pity it's not yours,' Pete muttered as Gerald left the room.

Bogart marched in seconds later. 'There are a few slivers of bacon left,' he said, 'plus half a dozen hash browns and the odd sausage.'

'Any even ones?' Pete asked.

Bogart frowned. 'I'm sorry?'

'Never mind, just put it all on a plate and I'll try and make do.'

'Any croissants?' Angie asked.

'No. Cereals, juices, tea and coffee are over there.'

Angie went to inspect the jugs and bowls on a side-table. 'Mum still playing maids?' I asked the Golden Oldies as Pete and I sat down.

'She is,' said Audrey. 'And very well too.'

'Damn sight better than at home,' said Dad. 'I'll have to get her a uniform.'

When they got up to go, Audrey told us that the inspector was coming back soon to continue his investigations.

'Can we skip that?' I asked.

'Not a chance,' my dad said. 'If we have to be there, so do you.'

When the three of us were alone, Pete said, 'Village?'

'Good plan,' I said.

Pete and I would have snuck out right after shovelling down our fodder, but Angie marched us upstairs to clean our teeth first.* Ten minutes later, as we were leaving the house, the lopsided gardener came along pushing his wheelbarrow. He didn't have his cap on this time. The hair the cap had covered looked like it was made out of an old horse's tail. It was not great hair.

'Morning, Mr Blackberry,' said Pete.

'Blackthorrn,' the gardener snapped.

'Blackcurrant?' Pete said.

Wheelbarrow Man narrowed his eyes. 'Black-*thorrn*. You deaf, boy?'

---

* We cleaned our own.

Pete cupped his ear. 'What was that, Mr Blackball?'

'Pete, get it right, will you?' I said, stepping in. 'It's Black*bean*.'

Mr B flipped to me. 'Black-*thorrn*,' he growled.

'That's what I said,' I replied. 'Blackbird.'

He ground his teeth. 'Black-*thorrn*!'

'All right, all right, we get it,' said Pete. 'Black*board*, OK?'

'No! Black-*THORRN*!'

'No need to shout, Mr Blacksmith,' I said.

Hands gripped the backs of Pete's neck and my neck. Angie's hands.

'Sorry about these two, Mr Blackthorn. They have this infant mentality problem. I'll take them out of your hair.'

'Wig, you mean,' said Pete as she steered us away. 'A blind mole could've spotted it.'

We set off along the drive, running low to avoid Golden Oldie radar. Only when the house was hidden by trees did we start walking like fully evolved bipeds. The sign at the end of the drive told us that the village of Haddenuff was a quarter-mile away, though it felt a lot longer when we walked it. The village turned out to be a single street lined with cottages, bungalows and small houses. There were a few parked vehicles, men thatching a roof, a couple of women sniffing flowers in a garden and a man lifting trays out of a red and yellow van with 'Haddenuff Catering' on the side. And that was it.

'You said there'd be a sweet shop,' Pete said to Angie.

'No, I said there'd probably be nothing *but* a sweet shop.'

'And a vandalised phone box and a broken-down tractor,' I said. 'I see no such things.'

'There's a pub,' she said.

'They wouldn't let us in,' said Pete.

'I know. I'm clutching at straws here.'

'Sport all afternoon,' I said.

'What?' said Ange.

I indicated a notice in the window of The Haddenuff Hawker which said there'd be live sport all Saturday afternoon on a seventy-inch TV.

'Wouldn't think there'd be enough sporty types in a dead-and-alive hole like this to bother with a screen of *any* size,' said Pete.

'What's going on down there?' Angie said, nodding towards the far end of the village, where people were doing stuff.

'Who cares?' I said.

'I'm going to see.'

And she was off. Pete and I followed, the way we

always seem to follow Angie, but ultra-casually so people wouldn't know we were ruled by a woman. What we found at the end of the village was people putting up big tents in a field and men hammering nails into wood. Pete and I would have watched all this for four and a half seconds max, but Angie had to know the whole story and she went into the field to find out. A couple of the wood hammerers stopped work and chatted to her for a bit. She came back with a piece of paper they'd given her.

'They're setting up for a village fete tomorrow,' she said.

'Ooh, murder weekends *and* village fetes,' said Pete sarcastically.

'I like village fetes,' said Ange.

'When did you ever go to a village fete?' I asked.

'I went to one a few years back when me and Mum were staying with my aunt and uncle in the country. It was cool.'

'Some people,' Pete said. 'So easy to please.'

I flicked the piece of paper in Angie's hand. 'And this is?'

'A flyer advertising the fete.'

'Let's see.'

'Why, so you can mock, like Garrett?'

'Naturally.' I snatched it off her, and read what

75

was printed on it – aloud. "'The annual Haddenuff Village Fete will once again have all the attractions visitors have come to expect, such as cheese rolling, a coconut shy, pig races, home-made ginger beer and the ever-popular children's entertainer Tommy Rotter. Mr Marconi (The Codfather) will be here as ever with his Traditional Fish and Chips.'"

'Chips,' said Pete, brightening.

'But not today,' said Angie.

I carried on reading. "'Unfortunately, for the first time in our fete's thirty-five-year history, there'll be no morris dancing. This popular event has been banned by Health and Safety, who fear that one dancer's quarterstaff might accidentally rap another's knuckles, or a toe get bruised inside an over-enthusiastic clog. That depressing news aside, roll up, roll up, from ten o'clock this Sunday for the fete of the year.'"

'Haddenuff,' said Pete as I finished. 'Talk about well named, cos I have. Let's go.'

'Where?' said Angie.

'The house, where else?'

'The house means the murder weekend.'

'Yeah, I know, but...' Pete sighed.

'I suppose we'll just have to get through it,' I said. 'It's only for the rest of today and half of tomorrow anyway.'

'A lifetime,' said Pete. 'It wouldn't be *so* bad if I could get a signal on my phone. I could shut the murder stuff out and play some games then.'

'Tell you what we're gonna do,' said Angie as we started back. 'We're going to show the Golden Oldies how it's done.'

'How what's done?' I asked.

'We're going to solve their rotten murder in double-quick time, and as soon as we get home we're going to forget any of this ever happened.'

'It's obvious who did it,' said Pete. 'Bollinger.'

'We can't be sure of that,' I said.

'No? After what his girlfriend told us through the drainpipe?'

'That could've been to throw us off the scent.'

'She didn't know we were on the scent. She couldn't have. She was down there on the ground and we were up there in the clouds.'

'She must have known. They both must have. Why would two characters have a conversation about the murder of a pretend father if they didn't know they were being overheard?'

'Maybe in *case* we were listening,' said Pete.

'Well, I don't think it was him,' I said. 'Don't forget, someone else came on the scene after he hoofed it.'

'Oh, yes, the man you saw,' said Angie. 'But you didn't see his face.'

'No, just his hat.'

'It could have been a red herring.'

'No, it was definitely a hat.'

'He could have come on the scene just then to make us *think* he was the murderer.'

'Maybe, maybe not.' I reached for my free pen and notepad. 'I'd better write down our thinking so far,' I said.

'We don't need notes to keep track of this rubbish,' Angie said scornfully.

'No, course not. Kidding.'

I left the pen and pad where they were. We trudged back to the house.

CHAPTER EIGHT

We were on our way up the tree-lined drive when we heard a scuffling sound, and a man's chuckle, followed by a womanish giggle. Pete and I swerved in that direction, but Angie jumped behind a bush. No spying on couples making out for Angie Mint! We crept forward tree by tree (on the ground) until we could see the chuckler and the giggler in a clinch behind another one. It was quite a surprise to find that the chuckler was Bogart the butler, but even more of one to see that the giggler was...

'Mum!'

Yes, Peg McCue, my trusty mother.

'Jiggy!' She straightened her maid's uniform in haste.

'What are you doing?' I demanded, like I didn't know.

'Oh, we're just...admiring this tree.'

'Mother, is that really the best you can do?'

'Jig,' she said, 'it's not what you think.'

'Oh, no, so what is it then?'

'Larry and I...'

'Larry?'

'Mr Bogart. We were just...'

I held my palm up. 'Save it. Don't want to hear it. Now I know why you're so keen on your drama group. I bet Dad would like to know too.'

'Who was it?' Angie asked when Pete and I joined her at her bush.

'My mother,' I said. 'Necking the butler.'

'No!'

'Yep.'

For a minute the three of us just crouched there, trying to take it in.

But then...

'Hang on,' I said. 'She called him Bogart.'

'So?' said Pete.

'He's an actor playing a part. The part he's playing is Bogart the butler. That can't be his real name too.'

'Well, it *could*,' said Angie.

'Unlikely, though,' said Pete.

'Exactly,' I said. 'So why would she call him by the name of his part?'

'Better than calling him by a more private one,' said Pete.

'This is serious, Garrett. How would you like it if your mum...'

I trailed off. His mum had done the same thing way back, though not with a butler or behind a tree. All he saw of her these days was the occasional photo from Canada.

'Sorry,' I said.

'Yeah,' he said, kicking the ground.

'Maybe they're still in character,' said Angie as we carried on to the house. 'Like Honor and Rudy under the drainpipe. Maybe they have to be for the entire weekend. One of Roderick's rules.'

'Hmm...' I said.

It was a better thought than the one that had been jogging round my imagination with its arms folded over its head.

'Waaaaaaaaaaaaaa!'

'What's that?' said Angie.

'Well, if it isn't a piercing scream,' said Pete, 'it's a fair imitation of one.'

Then we heard a thump, like something heavy hitting the ground. The scream stopped.

Pause.

Then running feet.

Then cries of horror.

'Oh, my God! My God!'

We strolled to the corner of the house and peered round it. Audrey, Belinda Prosser, Myrtle the maid

81

and Lady Helga were stooping over Honor Naffington, who lay face down on the ground with a red puddle around her head.

'My darling!' Lady Helga cried.

'I'm guessing another fake murder,' Angie whispered.

'I saw her up on the roof a minute ago, my lady,' we heard Myrtle say. 'She must have slipped and fallen.'

'What's that in her hand?' said Audrey.

'Do we care?' said Pete.

We didn't. We backed away and went into the house.

'I'm going up to strip my bed,' Angie said as we crossed the hall.

'I'm going to the games room to see if I can beat myself at table tennis,' said Pete.

'I'm gonna find my dad,' I said as me and Ange went upstairs.

'You're not going to tell him about your mum and Bogart?'

'I might. Dunno yet.'

I wasn't sure what I would say to him actually, or even why I wanted to see him, I just felt... I don't know. What I did know was that finding Mum and Bogart in a clinch had stewed my prunes, big time. They might have still been in character like Angie said, but what if they weren't? What if...

I didn't really expect to find Dad in his room, but he was – sitting on the floor, cross-legged, eyes shut, doing the thumb-and-forefinger-on-the-knees thing. He looked calmer than he usually did by a long way, not moving a muscle or twitching a hair – until one eyelid flipped up and the half of his face on that side scowled.

'What?'

'How'd you know I was here?' I asked.

'I sensed you.'

'What are you doing?'

'Meditating, what does it look like?'

'How's it going?'

He closed the eye. 'It was going quite well till someone started asking damn fool questions like "How's it going?" Now can I get back to finding my inner cretin as recommended by the relaxation therapist forced on me by your certifiable mother?'

I stepped further into the room. 'It was Mum I wanted to talk to you about.'

Keeping his eyes closed and fingers and thumbs joined, he took a deep slow breath. 'What about her?'

'Is she still in character? I mean is she acting her part the whole time?'

'She hasn't said.'

'Well you must know, if anyone does,' I said. 'Was

she Mum or a maid when she went to bed last night?'

'No idea, she didn't sleep here. The Pure Isle Players have accommodation in another part of the house.'

'Oh. Right. So she probably is.'

'Is what?'

'Still in character. They must all be.'

'If you say so. Close the door on your way out.'

I'd almost got it closed when a voice rang out from the hall below.

'Everyone down here please! Everyone down here!'

The phoney policeman, Inspector Qwerty.

'God's codpiece,' groaned my father behind the almost closed door.

I heard footsteps rattling down the attic stairs. 'Think we're going to be told about Honor,' I said to Angie when she appeared.

Oliver came out of his and Audrey's room. 'Now what?' he said.

'Ask the inspector,' I said.

He leaned over the balcony. 'What's all the fuss?' he shouted down.

The inspector looked up. 'There's been another fatality, sir. I'd be obliged if all of you would come down.'

Dad stomped out of his room. He no longer had either of his eyes shut.

'It is *impossible* to be *calm* round here!' he growled.

Belinda, Audrey and the actor playing Rudy Bollinger were already in the hall by the time we got down, and Billy Prosser joined us half a minute later. Rudy stood next to a potted plant staring at the floor murmuring, 'I can't believe it. I can't believe it,' just loudly enough for us to hear. Lady Helga, sobbing dramatically, was being comforted by Myrtle on one of the couches.

'The stage is set,' Angie said to me.

She said it quietly, but the inspector heard. 'Not quite. We're not all here. Mr *Tozer* for one.' He said 'Tozer' like it wasn't a name he planned to forget this side of Christmas.

My mother the maid, whose uniform was too rumpled for my liking, came in the front door. 'What's happened?'

'Murder number two,' said Oliver.

The inspector wheeled on him. 'I said nothing of murder, sir!'

'Well, of course it's murder,' snapped my dad. 'What else could it be on a murder mystery weekend, death by exposure to peace and bloody *quiet*?'

Mum kept her distance from me, but when Bogart slipped in from the garden I saw her flutter her eyelids at him. He didn't flutter his back, or even glance in her direction.

The inspector took up a position in front of us, hands behind his back.

'It's my sad duty to inform those of you who don't already know,' he said, super-seriously, 'that Miss Honor Naffington has fallen from the roof and is no longer of this world.'

'Ooooooohhhhhh!' wailed Lady Helga. Myrtle gave her an extra cuddle.

'What was she doing on the roof?' asked Billy Prosser.

'I really can't say,' the inspector replied. 'As for how she came off it, my first thought was that she slipped, my second that she jumped.'

'Jumped?' said Rudy Bollinger. 'Are you suggesting that she committed suicide, Inspector? Honor wouldn't have done that, we were going to be married.'

'That could be why,' muttered Oliver.

'Married?' said Lady Helga, drying her eyes on something lacy.

'Yes, Helga, dear,' said Rudy, going to her and taking her hand. 'Just yesterday I asked Honor to be my wife, and she very generously consented. We were going to tell you last night, but then Sir Duff was so cruelly taken from us, and...well, the time clearly wasn't right.'

'Oh, my dear, my dear,' Lady H said, reaching for his

head and ramming it into her chest without so much as a by-your-leave. 'How I would have *adored* having you as my son-in-law! But now, alas, it can never be, oh-oh-oh.'

With this she broke down again, slobbering all over his hair.

'What a ham,' Angie whispered.

'If I may continue...?' the inspector said. When no one objected, he went on. 'Whatever I imagined initially – whether Miss Honor slipped or took her own life in grief following her father's assassination – I'm now obliged to recognise the possibility that she too is a homicide victim.'

Rudy Bollinger jerked his head off Lady H's chest.

'But who would murder my adorable Honor? Who? Who?'

'What's occurring?' Pete was suddenly standing with us.

'Bad dialogue and worse acting,' Angie whispered. 'How was the ping-pong?'

'I won.'

'That's what we're here to decide,' the inspector said in answer to Rudy's owl impression. 'Only one thing's for sure, and that is that the killer is someone in this house, either a member of the household, of the staff, or...'

He trailed off, staring round at us to make sure we knew that we were all suspects.

'I bet the butler did it,' said Ollie. 'The butler usually does it in efforts like this, and that one looks pretty dodgy to me.'

Bogart drew himself up and tried to look aloof, but the aloofness was kind of spoiled by his rumpled collar and the leaf in his hair.

'It can't have been him,' I said. 'He was...' – I glared at my mother – '...in the garden when Honor took her dive. We saw him.'

'Perhaps it was the cook,' Belinda Prosser piped up in her little girl voice.

'Cook?' said Audrey. 'We haven't seen the cook. At least, I haven't.'

'You wouldn't have,' a voice said from the back of the hall. Roderick stood in a corner. 'A private catering firm's handling the food.'

'*Whoever* the culprit turns out to be,' the inspector said, 'it might be that we have a clue to his or her guilt.'

'A clue!' squeaked Belinda. 'Oh, how exciting. What is it?'

The inspector took a transparent sandwich-type bag from his pocket and held it up. 'Seen anything like this before?'

'A plastic bag?' said Dad. 'Hey, yeah, think I've seen

one of those somewhere.'

The inspector frowned. 'Its *contents*,' he said.

Everyone leaned forward. The bag contained some small white flowers with red-tipped stalks.

'Aren't they the flowers found on Sir Duff's body?' Angie asked.

'Not quite,' said the inspector. 'Same variety, but these were in Miss Honor's hand when she fell. Now what does that suggest, I wonder?'

No one volunteered any thoughts.

'What it suggests to *me*,' the inspector went on, 'is that the killer is leaving a calling card, which begs the questions, why a flower, and why this *particular* flower?'

'Maybe it's his favourite,' said Audrey.

'Odd choice if so. There are more attractive blooms than the blackthorn.'

'Blackthorn?' said Angie. 'It's called a blackthorn?'

The inspector nodded. 'I'm something of a horticulturist off duty. Amateur, of course, but it's an abiding interest.'

Angie, Pete and I made eye contact. 'So he is one of them,' Angie said.

'No question,' I said.

'Do we tell them?'

'Oh, *please*,' said Pete. 'Let's get this *over* with.'

'We know who did it,' Angie said, for all three of us.

'You know who killed Sir Duff and Miss Honor?' said the inspector.

'Yep. The gardener.'

'Gardener?' said Oliver. 'I didn't know there was a gardener. Did you know there was a gardener, Mel?'

Dad shook his head. 'But even in a lousy Agatha Christie's Parrot set-up, the gardener seems a bit obvious with both victims holding flowers.'

'It's not just that he's a gardener,' Angie said. 'It's his name.'

'His name?' said the inspector.

'Same as the flower. He calls himself Mr Blackthorn.'

'Silas Blackthorn,' I added in case anyone was interested.

Dad laughed. 'Blackthorn? Oh, come on. A character and a clue with the same name? How could we ever have joined those dots if we didn't even know the man existed?'

'You should stop meditating and get out more,' I told him.

We left them talking among themselves and went up to our attic. We didn't want to go there, but as we'd just solved two murders a swift exit seemed the way to go for dramatic effect, and the attic was the only place we could all agree on without taking a vote.

CHAPTER NINE

We went out onto our bit of roof to see if we could locate Blackthorn the fake gardener from the battlements. We spotted him right away, pushing his wheelbarrow.

'He never seems to do any actual gardening,' said Angie.

'They probably don't teach gardening at acting school,' I said.

'You think this bunch *learned* acting?' said Pete.

'There they go!' Angie said.

Inspector Qwerty was marching towards old Silas followed by Audrey, Belinda, Myrtle and Rudy Bollinger. Blackthorn set down his wheelbarrow as they approached. We couldn't hear what was said from way up there, but when the inspector flipped him round, handcuffed his wrists and headed back to the house with him, again followed by the others, the result was pretty obvious.

'I wonder what the inspector will do with him?' Angie said.

'*Pretend* to do with him,' I said.

'He should torture him,' said Pete. 'For real. I'd like to see that.'

'So what do we do now the murderer's unmasked?' Angie again.

'Maybe they'll take us home,' I said.

'Home? You think?'

'Well, there's not a whole lot of point staying here with the murders solved, is there?'

To pass the time we rooted around the attic looking for stuff to do, which ended with Angie starting a cardboard jigsaw with a picture of a snowy mountain, me picking things up and putting them down, and Pete winding up clockwork locomotives and crashing them into one another. Silence for a while apart from the cosy sound of crashing trains, until Angie said, 'You don't think we're expected to work out his motive?'

'Whose?' I asked.

'Blackthorn's. He must've had a reason for killing Sir Duff and Honor.'

'Maybe his character resents working for toffs.'

'Nah, too easy.'

'Who says it has to be hard?'

'True. God, this is a boring jigsaw.'

'Not half as boring as what I'm doing,' I said.

'You're not doing anything.'

'Exactly. Wonder when lunch is?'

'I'm guessing around lunchtime.'

I looked at my watch. 'It's almost half-twelve.'

'Lunch might not be till one.'

'One for all,' I said.

'What?' she said.

'And all for lunch.'

'Shut up, McCue.'

Suddenly we heard a distant gong. Angie tipped the jigsaw back in its box without bothering to break up the bits she'd interlocked.

'One more crash,' said Pete as Ange and I headed for the stairs.

We watched two more engines chug round the track at the speed of snails, smash into one another, fall sideways.

'OK,' said Pete.

We went down.

In the dining room we found a buffet laid out on the long table with a stack of empty plates for us to help ourselves. No maid service, no butler. The only guests present were Dad, Oliver and Billy Prosser, who were strolling silently along the table picking out stuff they liked the look of or had to have because it was all there was. 'Still no chips,' said Pete.

'Quiet in here,' Angie said to the adults.

'There's not a lot to say now that three young smart-arses have solved the case that was meant to be strung out till tomorrow,' said my dad.

'We weren't expected to keep quiet when we knew the killer's identity, were we?' Angie said.

'S'pose not. I thought murder weekends were meant to keep you guessing right to the end. This one needs quite a bit more thought if it's going to work.'

'They ought to shelve the whole idea and go back to amateur dramatics,' I said.

'Amateur's right,' said Oliver. 'They don't know what acting is.'

'He used to do a bit,' Pete told Billy. 'Before I was born. The Dark Ages.'

'Dark Ages or not,' said Ollie, 'I could still show this crew a thing or two.'

Pete grabbed a fistful of ham and crammed it in his trap. 'I'm thinking chips,' he said round the ham. 'Mm-mm, great chips, yum-yum.'

'You're a real peasant, aren't you, Garrett?' Angie said.

'*Great* chips,' he said.

I was dropping dinky little sausage rolls on a plate and Angie was loading weeds on another when Gerald Tozer burst in.

'He refuses to confess!' he said like he was announcing a lottery win.

'Who does?' said Oliver.

'The gardener, under interrogation.'

'I didn't know you knew he'd been accused,' said Billy Prosser.

'I was poking around the garden when the inspector nabbed him,' Gerald said. 'Trying to find some flowers like the ones planted on Sir Duff.'

'And did you?'

'No. That man. I wasn't aware he even *existed* until I saw the inspector cuffing him.'

'You weren't the only one,' said Dad.

'Where did you hear about him not confessing?' Oliver asked Gerald.

'The butler chappy, who was told by Qwerty. Maybe he'll weaken after lunch. The gardener, I mean.' He went back to the door, all bright-eyed and eager. 'I'll go see if I can glean anything else.' He went out.

'No confession,' sighed Dad. 'Which probably means they'll milk it all the way to this time tomorrow.'

'Gawd 'elp us,' said Oliver.

'It wouldn't be *so* bad,' Dad said, 'if you could get a decent drink round here. There's not a drop of beer on the premises, even in bottles.'

'Wonder if there's a pub in the vicinity?' said Ollie.

'There's one in Haddenuff,' said Pete round another gobful of ham.

'Haddenuff?'

'Village down the road. We went there earlier.'

'To the pub?'

'The village.'

'There's a big TV screen too,' I said.

'In the village?'

'The pub. Showing sport all afternoon.'

Ollie glanced at Dad. 'Mel?'

'You bet.' Dad turned to me. 'You won't tell your mother?'

'I'm not talking to that woman ever again,' I said. 'She's out of my will.'

'Good lad.'

'Or Audrey,' said Oliver to Angie.

She crossed her heart. 'Where is Mum anyway?' she asked.

'She and my wife took some food into the garden,' said Billy Prosser.

'If they're in full chat mode they might not miss us anyway,' Dad said. 'How far's this village?'

'Twenty minutes, half an hour,' I said.

'Half an hour? By car?'

'Walking.'

'Two minutes tops then. Care to join us?' Dad said to Billy.

Billy shook his head. 'Making a phone call was bad enough. Dread to think what'd happen if I went to a pub this early in the marriage.'

Dad and Oliver abandoned their half-empty plates and walked out looking quite a bit more pleased with life than when we came in. As Billy was the only one left and we had nothing to say to him we left in a minute too, me stuffing sausage rolls in my pocket, Pete with two fistfuls of crustless sandwiches. Angie, because she's Angie, patted her stomach like she'd just thrown a massive feast into it, and took nothing.

In the hall we found Myrtle polishing the piano. Standing up on top of the piano, like it had been put there specially, was *Latin Names of Common Flowers*. It sure got about, that book.

'You can stop now, it's all over,' Pete said to Myrtle.

'Pardon me, young sir?' she said, all innocent and maidish in spite of her age.

'OK, play it out to the bitter end if you have to.'

We went to the front door, and out to the garden. We had nothing to do in the garden, so we just mooched. Hither and thither we mooched. Then we mooched hither and yon for a change. Mooching was getting to be quite a pain by the time we came to the secret garden door that Angie had liked the look of on our last tour. 'I have to see what's in there,' she said.

'I'd bet good money there's nothing,' said Pete.

'You haven't got any money, good or bad,' said Angie.

'No, but if I had I'd bet it.'

Angie jerked the latch. The door didn't want to open at first, but when she put her shoulder against it, it moved, and another push did the trick.

'I said there was nothing,' said Pete, peering in.

There really wasn't. The empty wheelbarrow, a few defeated-looking apple trees, some chipped chimney pots, a couple of lidless dustbins, bits of junk and scrap, a heap of bricks, a wooden crate on old pram wheels.

'A go-cart,' said Pete, running the crate back and forth to try it out. 'Push me, someone,' he said, slotting himself into it.

I put my foot on the back of the cart and shoved. The wheels squealed, and the thing moved a little way and ran into the heap of bricks.

Pete climbed out. 'Let's take it outside. There are slopes out there. I want to go down a slope.'

'You'll break your neck,' said Ange.

'Let's do it,' I said.

Pete lugged the cart out to a grassy slope and

climbed back in. I kicked the back of the thing.

'Wheeeeee!' said Pete, going down.

He expected to ride all the way to the bottom, but the slope dipped halfway, the cart tipped sideways, and –

'Waaaaaah!'

– he was lying across the graves we'd come across last night: Keith and Sylvia's. Not for long, though. He was up in an instant, shaking his arms in horror, smacking earth off himself like it was contaminated. Then he grabbed the cart and lugged it back through the door in the wall.

'Kids these days,' said Angie. 'No staying power.'

Back in the unsecret garden I plucked an apple from one of the twisted old trees, polished it on a sleeve and sank the McCue choppers into it (the apple).

'Are you sure you want to do that?' Angie asked me.

'Do what?'

'Eat that apple. It has to have been hanging there since last year.'

'It's fine,' I said, but before I'd finished the chunk in my mouth it went a bit off. I looked at the apple in my hand. Something was wriggling in the hollow my teeth had carved.

Half a maggot.

Which meant the other half…

I dropped the apple and spat and spat and spat, and when I was all spat out I snatched the last two sausage rolls from my pocket and crammed them into my mouth to try and cover the taste and thought of maggot. I'd tasted live maggot once before and hadn't planned to ever repeat the experience in this lifetime, and I'd just done that very thing.*

I was still madly chewing sausage roll when there was a distant yell.

'What was that?' Angie said.

'Sounded like a yell,' said Pete. 'A distant one.'

'Let's check it out.'

She ran through the door and almost knocked someone flying. Gerald Tozer. 'Whoa!' he said like she was a horse. 'Steady, steady!'

'Sorry,' said Ange. 'Did you hear a shout just now?'

'Yes. From down there. That's where I was headed, to see what was up.'

We set off, all four of us. The yell wasn't repeated, but we heard voices, which we tracked to the lily pond. They belonged to Inspector Qwerty, Rudy Bollinger, Belinda Prosser and Audrey Mint. They were standing over a very wet person on the ground. Rudy and the inspector were damp from the waist down. The even wetter person on the ground was

---

* To hear about Jiggy's previous maggot munch, read a book called *The Meanest Genie*. But here's a tip for the squeamish: DON'T!

Larry Bogart the butler.

'What happened?' asked Gerald.

'Mr Bollinger and I dragged him out of the water,' the inspector said.

'What was he doing in the water?'

'Drowning. Of course, he could have fallen in by accident, but...'

'But?' said Belinda. She sounded just a bit excited.

'I suspect that we have another murder on our hands!'

CHAPTER TEN

'*Another* murder?' Angie said. 'Has Blackthorn escaped then?'

'Indeed he has not,' the inspector said. 'He's handcuffed to the radiator in the library. One of the old kind, solid iron, immovable.'

Gerald beamed. 'They always handcuff them to that kind of radiator.'

'Only in really naff or old-fashioned stories,' I muttered.

'I was taking a break from questioning him when these ladies' cries alerted me,' said the inspector. He turned to Audrey and Belinda. 'What were you doing here anyway?'

'Just taking a turn round the garden,' Audrey said. 'First chance we've had really.'

'And we heard the sound of a struggle,' said Belinda, 'then a splash, and more struggles, then someone pushed by us, and we turned the corner and saw Mr Bogart face down in the water.'

'Who pushed by you?' the inspector asked.

'Don't know, he was so quick, and he wore a hat and had his head down.'

'Jig saw a man in a hat last night,' Angie said, shoving me forward.

'Oh?' The inspector swivelled to me. 'Did you see his face?'

I glared at Angie. 'No. I only saw him from above. The hat got in the way.'

'Well, that doesn't get us very far, does it?' he said irritably. 'So, now we have three deaths and an unseen killer still at large.'

'And those,' said Gerald Tozer, pointing at Bogart's soggy buttonhole. There was a tiny bunch of very familiar flowers in it.

'I don't get it,' said Audrey. 'These flowers. Three lots now. But if Blackthorn the gardener isn't the culprit...'

'Yes, it's a puzzle, isn't it?' the inspector said.

I took Pete aside. 'Maybe my dad did it.'

'Did what?'

'Killed Bogart. He might have heard about Bogart snogging Mum.'

'Jig,' he said. 'Bogart isn't really dead. Besides, your dad's at the pub.'

'Yes. I know. But still.' I glared at the wet body on the ground. 'Wonder if he could still play dead if

I kicked him in the ribs?'

'Give it a go,' said Pete.

It was tempting, but there'd be witnesses.

'There aren't that many left who could be the killer with Blackthorn out of the picture,' said Gerald. 'Just the two maids, Lady H and Mr Bollinger here.'

'Well, it wasn't *me*!' Rudy said indignantly. 'I might not have had much love for the old man, but Honor had agreed to marry me, and I had nothing against the butler.'

'Honor hadn't agreed to marry you,' said Angie.

'What? She had. And how would you know anyway?'

'We were on the roof last night, top of the tower, when you two were having a row.'

'Row? Me and Honor? Nonsense. And I've never been on the tower.'

'You were down below. We heard Honor accuse you of killing her dad and threaten to expose you to the inspector today.'

The inspector turned to Rudy with interest. 'Oh, did she now?'

'No, she did not,' said Rudy. 'If these kids heard anything, it was someone else. I didn't go out last night.'

'Don't believe him, inspector,' said Ange. 'It was him all right.'

Pete and I raised an eyebrow at one another. One

each. Angie was starting to sound like the others. Should we grab her by the armpits and drag her away before she got totally involved?

'Rudy left the library just before Sir Duff was shot,' Angie went on, 'and he was worried that Honor would mention it to you. Where was he when Bogart copped it?'

'I met him on the way here,' the inspector said.

'Oh, come *on*!' Rudy snapped. 'What possible reason could I have for killing a butler?'

'You might have had a reason or you might not,' the inspector said, 'but I'll be asking you to account for your movements, Mr Bollinger. First, however, I must get forensics here.'

With the inspector in the lead, all of us (except Bogart) headed for the house. Rudy looked steaming mad. Audrey and Belinda grinned at one another. Gerald whispered to us that he thought it was all 'rather thrilling'.

At the house, the inspector went to the telephone table and grabbed the old-fashioned receiver. I couldn't hear what he said – he spoke very quietly – but I did catch the word 'forensics'.

'How's it going, Inspector?' a cheery voice said as he hung up. Roderick, sticking his head out of a side room.

'Not so well, sir, since you ask,' the inspector replied

in his best phoney cop manner. 'A further body's been discovered.'

'A *further* body?' said Rod in equally phoney horror. 'You don't mean…'

'Yes. Another murder appears to have been committed.'

'By Jove, how shocking. Well, let's hope you find the culprit pdq, eh?'

'Yes, sir, indeed, sir.'

Roderick pulled his head back into the room and closed the door.

'What'll happen to Mr Blackthorn?' Angie asked the inspector.

'He'll be released without charge. The rest of you will remain on the premises in case I wish to question you.' He opened the library door. 'Mr Bollinger?'

'Can I get out of these wet clothes first?' Rudy asked.

'Later,' the inspector said. 'In here, if you please, sir.'

'Perhaps I should have a lawyer present.'

'Up to you, sir, but if you've nothing to hide, why would you need a lawyer?'

Rudy barged angrily past him. 'Very well, let's get it over with.'

As the inspector closed the door behind them, I took out my complimentary pen and notebook.

'*Now* do I make some notes?' I said.

'No,' said Angie.

I put the pen and pad away.

While Gerald, Audrey and Belinda flopped onto the couches round the fireplace, we parked ourselves in big bulgy chairs well away from them. On a small table between us was that book that kept changing locations, *Latin Names of Common Flowers*. After a minute Billy Prosser came downstairs and joined Belinda and the others. The four of them went into an immediate huddle.

'They're really getting into this,' said Ange.

'So were you back at the pond,' said Pete.

'I was just giving it a whirl to see how it felt.'

'And?'

'It was OK.'

'Wonder where Blackthorn went?' I said. 'The inspector said he left him handcuffed to a radiator in the library, but he just went in there with Rudy, and Blackthorn hasn't come out.'

Pete screwed his face up. 'Jig, are you losing it?'

'What do you mean?'

'He wasn't really handcuffed to the radiator. He was an actor playing a part, and his part's done. He's probably skived off somewhere, never to be seen again, by us anyway.'

'I know all that,' I said. 'I was just wondering, is all.'

After a while Rudy came out, scowling. 'Ask the maids to come in, Mr Bollinger!' the inspector shouted after him.

'I don't know where they are,' Rudy answered grumpily.

'Try the dining room.'

Rudy stalked to the dining room and looked in. He mumbled something and my mother and Myrtle came out, all wide-eyed and worried-looking. Rudy went in and closed the door after him. 'You knew it wasn't Blackthorn, didn't you?' I said to Mum as the two of them scurried to the library. She went all fluttery and ultra-maidish, but said nothing.

'Remind me never to go into amateur dramatics,' said Angie as they closed the library door.

'Never go into amateur dramatics, Ange,' I said.

'Thanks, Jig.'

'Suppose it's not one of the actors,' said Pete.

'Suppose what's not one of the actors?' I asked.

'The killer. I mean if we include Mona there's only four of them left, and if it's a man there's only Rudy. But how do we know they're the only characters?'

'Because there's no one else,' said Ange.

'There's Gerald,' said Pete. 'And the Prossers.'

'But they're guests, like us.'

'So we've been told. But being told something by a total stranger doesn't necessarily make it true. Suppose they're only pretending to be guests?'

Angie opened her mouth to argue, but stopped before words came. We looked towards the fireplace. The Prossers, Gerald Tozer and Audrey were still in close conversation.

'The Prossers can't be acting,' I said. 'They're so ordinary. 'Specially her.'

'Almost *too* ordinary,' said Pete.

'It's a thought,' said Angie. 'Though if I was going for an actor posing as a guest it would be Gerald. Too chirpy by half, that one. Almost over the top.'

'Maybe it's just the way he is,' I said.

'Yes. Maybe. And maybe we should talk to him.'

'And say what? If he's acting he's hardly going to admit it, is he?'

'Why are they looking at us?' said Pete.

They were too. All four of them. Then Gerald got up and came over. He fell into a spare chair near us.

'I was just telling the others something that you should know,' he said. 'I didn't speak up while we were down by the pond because…well, I didn't. But you know you mentioned overhearing Rudy and Honor having a set-to last night? Well, so did I.'

109

'How come?' I said.

'I went into the games room shortly after you did and saw that you weren't there. I was taking a solo turn at the dartboard when I heard voices outside the window. I sneaked closer to earwig and heard Honor say she was going to tell the inspector about Rudy not being with her and Her Ladyship when Daddy was shot.'

Angie glanced at me and Pete. 'Did you also hear the man in the hat after Rudy stormed off?' she asked Gerald.

'Well, I don't know if he wore a hat, I didn't see him, but I heard Honor ask someone what he was doing there and say something about him being after her money like all the others. All a bit stagey, if you ask me, a bit melodramatic, but my thinking is that it's not Rudy who's our murderer, but the latecomer, the second chap.'

'The man in the hat,' I said. 'Yeah, that's what I think.'

'Would you excuse us for a minute?' said Angie.

She hauled Pete and me out of our chairs and Gerald's earshot.

'He wouldn't be saying all that if he was one of the actors,' she whispered.

'He might,' whispered Pete.

'Well, I'm betting not. He seems to be genuinely keen on working this out. I vote we take a chance and tell him of our suspicions about the Prossers.'

'My suspicions,' said Pete.

'If the murderer's the man in the hat, there's no one left except one of the male guests, and the only male guest left apart from Gerald and the dads is...?'

'Billy Prosser,' I said.

'Right. And if Billy's an actor, then Belinda must be too. So do we tell him?'

We agreed and went back to Gerald.

'No!' he said in disbelief when we'd spilled our beans. 'But the Prossers are so...*normal.*'

'Yes,' said Angie. 'But are they *deliberately* normal, that's the question.'

'Deliberately normal?'

'To seem above suspicion.'

He shook his head. 'I find it hard to believe that those two are play-acting.'

'Maybe they're better actors than the others,' I said.

'Wouldn't be hard,' said Pete.

'Anyway, who else is there?' said Angie.

'Hmm...' Gerald mused. 'This should be tested. But before I try and tease it out of them...'

He took out the pen and pad Roderick had given him and started writing.

'What are you doing?' Pete asked.

'Jotting down these stimulating new thoughts.' He glanced up. 'Aren't you writing things down too?'

I might have answered this, but Angie glared at me. 'It's all in here,' she said, tapping the side of her head.

Gerald smiled. 'Ah, the sharp minds of youth.'

When he'd put the pad and pen away, Angie asked him if he'd let us know if he got anything out of the Prossers.

'Indeed I will.' Gerald grinned. 'Getting more interesting by the minute, isn't it?' He slapped his knees, got up and went back to the others.

We looked at one another. More interesting by the minute? We shook our heads. 'Interesting' was waaaay too big a word for it.

Still, it wasn't quite as boring as it had been.

CHAPTER ELEVEN

It was Angie who suggested going back to the lily pond to see if Bogart was still there.

'Why would he be?' I said.

'Well, he's supposed to be dead.'

'Yeah, but he's not really. There are no actual forensics people coming either.'

'Getting the hang of it at last, eh, Jig?' said Pete.

We went back to the pond anyway. Bogart wasn't there. All there was to say that he had been was a spot of damp where he'd been lying.

'Wherever he disappeared to,' Angie said, 'he's got to keep well out of sight from now on.'

'He's probably gone to the actors' quarters,' I said.

'Actors' quarters?'

'The Pure Isle Players have rooms somewhere else in the house. Dad told me. I'm thinking that that's where Roderick was coming from when we were nosing around outside yesterday.'

'Top of those curvy steps, you mean?'

'Yeah.'

'All right, let's take a look.'

'Why?'

'Cos I want to.'

So we went to the steps we'd seen Roderick jogging down the day before. Pete and I kept watch while Angie snuck up. Then she snuck down.

'Door's open,' she whispered.

'What did you do, kick it in?' Pete asked.

'It was ajar. Must be someone in there. Come on.'

And back up she went. Pete and I looked this way and that to make sure we weren't observed, then raced after her. She was looking through the open part of the door at the top. We looked too, and saw a small room with some doors off it, a few bits of furniture, a rack with some coats and a couple of hats. One of the hats could have been the one worn by the man at the drainpipe, our chief suspect.

Suddenly one of the doors opened and a man came in. Bogart. He picked up a magazine from a little table, and sat down in an armchair to flip through it.

'Someone else,' whispered Pete.

Another door had opened. A woman this time, in shadow at first.

'Not my mum, is it?' I said.

'Can't be,' Pete said. 'She's in the library with Myrtle and the inspector.'

'It's Lady Helga,' said Angie.

She was right. Lady H sank into another armchair and lit a cigarette.

'You know, this is just a teensy bit against the rules,' a voice said behind us.

We jumped round. Instant guilt and confusion.

Roderick smiled at us from his great height. 'Worry not. Curiosity's what this weekend's all about. But perhaps you should run along now?'

'Yes,' said Ange. 'Right. Running.'

He stood aside to allow us to barge past him and make ourselves as scarce as we knew how.

Dad and Ollie got back from the pub about half an hour before dinner. Their eyes were wandering a bit.

'How was the sport?' I asked them.

'Shport?' said Dad. 'What shport?'

'You didn't drive in that condition, did you?'

'No, he did.'

'That's because I can hold my bitter lequor,' said Oliver.

'Your bitter lequor?' said Angie.

'Liquor better. Are you drunk, Ange?'

'I can't believe you drove in that state,' she said. 'Have you no sense of responsibility?'

'Better not let Mum see you like this,' I said to Dad,

115

who was examining a spot on the wall that wasn't visible to eyes that hadn't been to a pub.

'I have nothing to say to Mona the moaning maid,' he said. 'She goshe her way an' I go...some other.'

'Think I'll take a nittle lap,' said Oliver.

'Is that a little nap?' said Pete.

'Absholutely,' said Ollie, starting upstairs and tripping over stair two.

'Shounds good to me,' said Dad, following him and tripping over stair one.

We watched this sad pair stagger upstairs, chortling quietly and holding the banisters like they'd tumble back down if they didn't, which they probably would have. Angie sighed. 'Dads. Whole other species.'

We went to the games room and did nothing much till we heard the dinner gong (don't know who worked it, never saw the gong) and went up to get the dads. They were asleep – in each other's rooms. We went down again and told Audrey, who wasn't thrilled.

'Well, they'll miss dinner and be hungry later,' she said, 'but that's their problem.'

'What if they're still asleep by the time you go to bed?' I asked.

'Then I kick your dad out and lock my door. Ollie can sleep it off on the landing.'

With the dads dozing upstairs there should have

been eight for dinner, but Roderick didn't turn up, so it was just Audrey, Gerald, Belinda, Billy, and us three. We were convinced by this time that the Prossers were part of the scam and kept a sharp eye out for signs of acting, but they gave nothing away. We didn't get a chance to ask Gerald if he'd picked up anything from their behaviour, but he winked at us across the table, which suggested that he had something to tell us. Whatever he had in mind, we never heard it, because as we were finishing our meal there were these agitated voices out in the hall, and Inspector Qwerty burst in, all bug-eyed like he'd just bumped into the ghost of his dead granny.

'There's been a murder!' he shouted.

'Oh, not another one,' groaned Pete.

'A fourth?' said Audrey. Even she looked like she'd had enough murders for one weekend.

'No, this is a real one,' the inspector said. 'It's... horrible!'

And he rushed back out.

'*Now* what are they up to?' Billy Prosser said.

'Oh, like you don't know,' said Angie.

'Sorry?' he said.

She might have told him that we'd got his number, but my mother ran in, still in her maid's outfit.

'Jiggy! Angie! Pete!'

'Mother,' I said. 'Mona would never call us by name. And you were doing so well too. Not bad, anyway, considering.'

'I want you three to go upstairs and stay there,' she said. 'This isn't for your eyes.'

Frowns round the table as she flew out. Then Gerald got up. 'Need to check on this,' he said, and also went.

Audrey and the Prossers weren't slow to follow Gerald, but we kids took our time. It was all so obviously part of the scheme to keep things moving and us guessing. When we sauntered out to the hall we found the others crowding the library doorway, chattering like loons. We sighed. Was there no *end* to this?

'Let's wake the dads,' said Angie. 'They should suffer this if we have to.'

Dad and Oliver, in the wrong rooms, stirred when we shook them, said, 'Wossup?' and would have turned over if we hadn't hauled them onto the floor.

'You have to go downstairs. Guess what? Murder's afoot.'

The three of us changed our minds about going back down, but because there was a shortage of other places to go, we went to our attic. We kicked our heels for a while, then kicked each other's, then Pete went back to the clockwork train set, Angie started flicking through some of the old books on the shelves, and I pulled out a dusty old draughts board and defeated myself at draughts with three pieces missing.

'I'm going onto the roof,' Angie said after a while.

After another while I went out too. Angie wasn't there, which was kind of puzzling as there was nowhere to go except over the battlements. I remembered what had supposedly happened to Honor Naffington and went to check. No, she wasn't down there on the ground, all spread-eagled in a pool of blood.

'Jig! Up here!'

Angie was looking down at me from the top of the tower.

'How'd you get up there?'

'How many guesses do you want? Come on. Something you gotta see.'

Of course! We hadn't bolted the door when we were in the tower last night!

I opened the door and climbed the stairs and the little ladder. At the top, on the roof, Angie was leaning against the battlements, waiting for me.

'You know the chats we heard through the drainpipe?' she said.

'Yes…'

'And how we wondered if they were for our benefit, but couldn't see how they could know we were up here?'

'Yes…'

'I think they did.'

'Did what?'

'Know we were up here.' She squatted down beside the ciggie packet she'd spotted the previous night. 'Ever seen this brand before?'

'I don't smoke. I couldn't care less what brands there are.'

'OK, but look at this.'

She touched a small green circle that was part of the pack design.

'What am I looking at?' I asked.

'A spycam.'

'A what?'

'Miniature camera that transmits to some remote viewing station.'

'You're paranoid,' I said. 'What would a camera be doing up here? There's nothing to see.'

'There's us.'

'Us? No one knew we were going to be here. We didn't know ourselves.'

She straightened up. 'Cameras like this are cheap and disposable. They could be planted all over the place and no one would know.'

'So you think this one picked us up, passed the info to Rudy, Honor and the man in the hat, and they put that performance on just for us?'

She nodded. 'For us, and maybe for Gerald in the games room too.'

She brought her heel down on the fag packet, then tossed the crushed result over the battlements.

'Litterbug,' I said.

We went back down to our luxury penthouse apartment. Pete had got fed up of clockwork trains and lay on his bed with a pillow over his face, legs up the wall.

'Hey, yet *another* murder!' I said. 'Garrett's been suffocated.'

Angie yanked the pillow off his face. 'Up!' she said. 'We have some heavy searching to do.'

'Searching?'

'For spy cameras.'

She explained. At first Pete didn't believe anyone would stick tiny cameras all over the place, but when he saw how bothered Angie was by the possibility he joined us in searching the attic. We looked into everything, under everything, behind everything. We even checked out the manky old toilet, but found no evidence of tiny cameras anywhere.

'There might not be any here,' Angie said, 'but I'm getting changed under the blankets tonight just in case. Let's go downstairs.'

'And do what?' I said. 'Listen to more rubbish about fake murders?'

'It's either that or sit around here wondering if we're being watched.'

Halfway down the main stairs we heard the sound of an approaching siren. Below us, in the hall, everyone stood or sat around the fireplace – everyone except Roderick and Myrtle. Even the actors who'd played Honor Naffington and Bogart were present, and they looked very serious. They all did, not just the actors. Belinda Prosser was more than serious. She was sobbing quietly. Billy had his arm round her. Lady Helga seemed close to tears too, and Honor looked very pale. My mother and Audrey sat together on one of the couches, the inspector sat on the fireplace fender looking like he'd been kicked where it hurt, Gerald and Rudy leaned against the mantelpiece talking quietly, and even Dad and Oliver seemed to have sobered up.

'What's all this?' Angie asked.

'I was just coming to look for you,' said Audrey, jumping up and taking her hand. 'There's been a murder. None of us are safe here.'

Angie snatched her hand away. 'We know there's been a murder. We were with you at the table when the inspector and Peg rushed in.'

'You don't seem very shocked.'

'It's a murder mystery weekend,' Angie said. 'Murder's what happens at murder weekends, haven't you noticed?'

'This isn't part of the weekend,' said Gerald.

'What do you mean?'

'Roderick's been killed.'

'Boo-hoo-hoo,' blubbed Belinda P.

'Roderick?' I said.

'His head's been staved in,' my dad said, and when Ollie added, 'In the library,' Belinda wailed even louder.

The doorbell clanged. All eyes flipped doorward, but no one went to open it until the actor who'd played Bogart made a move. A man in a blue uniform stood on the step. The uniform had three stripes on the sleeve. He looked sort of familiar, but I couldn't place him. 'Who's in charge here?' he said, coming in.

'I am.'

We turned to see who'd spoken. It was Myrtle, coming out of the library. She was in ordinary clothes, not the maid's outfit, and she didn't look all shy and humble now. She walked briskly towards the sergeant.

'You're not alone, I hope,' she said.

'I'm all the station can spare,' he answered. 'Spate of burglaries around the village. And you are?'

'DCI Jane Smurfit,' said Myrtle. 'Talkington CID.'

'DCI?' I said to Bogart as he passed on his way back to the fireplace.

'Detective Chief Inspector,' he said. 'Her real-life persona.'

'Real-life?' said Pete.

'She's a copper?' said Angie.

'She is,' said Bogart. 'Quite handy her being a Pure Isle Player in the circumstances.'

CHAPTER TWELVE

Naturally, we didn't believe the new scenario. Why would we? Soppy old maid Myrtle a high-ranking cop? Actors coming back to life because someone had really been killed? Per-*lease*! The police sergeant's name didn't help convince us. Sergeant Fawkes. 'If his first name turns out to be Guy…' said Pete. Knowing this was just a little extra twist to the murder weekend deal, we Musketeers played along while making sure that knowing grins were never far from our features. 'One for all and all for lunch, eh?' I whispered to the others.

They stared at me blankly, like I'd just said, 'How are the pimples on your bum?' in Chinese.

'You're supposed to say it too,' I reminded them.

'I'm not in the mood,' said Ange.

'Me neither,' said Pete.

'Mood?' I said. 'Mood has nothing to do with it. "One for all and all for lunch" is what we say in times of adversity, or when we've triumphed over something or someone, or when the rest of the world is out of sync with us.'

'Well, I think I'll stick with the knowing grin this time around,' Angie said.

'Me too,' said Pete.

I would have had strong words to say to them about this, but just then DCI Smurfit, so-called, shunted the sergeant into the library, and Pete turned to the actors and said, 'When we got here, we found a noose in our room. A hangman's noose. What was that all about?'

It was the actress who'd played Honor who answered this. 'It was there for atmosphere.'

'To spook us, you mean,' Pete said.

'Oh, I wouldn't say that. More to set the scene really.'

'And the graves?' Angie said.

'Graves?'

'In the garden. Keith and Sylvia's.'

Honor knew nothing about any graves, but the one who'd played Rudy Bollinger said, 'Great Danes. The owners' dogs. They were killed when a contractor dropped a batch of tiles from a section of roof he was repairing.'

'Dogs,' said Pete, slapping his own face for not thinking of that.

'You two,' Angie said, turning to the Prossers. 'You might as well admit it now. You're part of the troupe, aren't you, and Billy's the murderer?'

'P-part of the troupe?' said the tearful Belinda.

'Me, the murderer?' said Billy.

Angie pointed at him, so melodramatically that you'd think she was auditioning for a part herself. 'You were the man in the hat. Don't bother to deny it. It had to be you who spoke to Honor after Rudy stormed away from the drainpipe, there's no other male left.'

'I have no idea what you're talking about,' Billy said.

'First I've heard of a man in a hat,' said Oliver.

'Or a drainpipe,' said my dad.

'You've never heard of a drainpipe?' I said to Dad. 'You really *do* need to get out more.'

'Prove you're really a guest,' Angie said to Billy.

'If I wasn't,' Billy said, 'what would be the point of keeping up the pretence when all the other actors are here now as their real selves?'

I jumped in. 'You said "other actors"! Not "*the* actors", "*other* actors", which proves you're one of them!'

'It proves no such thing,' Billy snapped. '*The* actors – satisfied?'

'All right, let's say you're who you claim to be,' said Angie. 'Anyone else care to admit to being the man in the hat?'

No one did. But Rudy said, 'I'm guessing it was my dad.'

'Your dad?'

'Roderick.'

'Roderick's your father?'

'Yes. Was, I should say. He often wore a hat.'

'But he said he wasn't acting this weekend,' Angie said.

'He could have been lying,' said Pete. 'That's what acting is, isn't it? Lying your socks off. Pretending. Making out.'

'Not making out,' I said grimly. 'That's what my mother does with butlers.'

'What's that, Jig?' said Dad.

I aimed a finger at Bogart. 'He was in a clinch with Mum behind a tree.'

'He what?'

'An oak,' said Angie. 'Least, I think it was. Might have been an elm – I'm not so hot on trees.'

My father turned to his wife. 'Peg?'

Mum's fingers were in knots, but she did a fair job of looking innocent. 'We were acting out our roles,' she said.

'Behind a tree?' said Dad.

'For the kids' benefit. We thought we'd give them something new to think about.'

'You did that all right,' I said.

'I have a murder weekend question,' said Audrey.

Eyes turned to her. 'Why did the gardener have the same name as the flower if he wasn't the killer?'

'I suppose we can tell them?' Honor said, eyeing the other actors.

'Doesn't matter one way or the other now,' said Bogart.

'It was hoped that someone would make the link between the flower's name and the gardener's,' Honor said. 'But if none of you had bumped into Blackthorn by late-afternoon today he would have made some excuse to come indoors and put his name about. However, the name was more of a hint than a clue.'

'A hint?' said Angie.

'It was intended to lead you to the Latin name of the flower,' said the actor who'd played the inspector and Sir Duff Naffington. (His real name, we heard soon after, was Reg Mote.)

'Latin name?'

'I'm sure you saw the book we kept relocating,' Reg said. '*Latin Names of Common Flowers*? We moved it every so often to make sure you all had a chance to notice it.'

'I didn't,' said Dad.

'Me neither,' said Oliver.

'Nor me,' said Billy.

'Or me,' said Pete.

'Jig and I did,' said Angie brightly.

'So did I,' sniffed Belinda, drying her eyes. 'Didn't pay it much attention, though.'

'I flipped through it,' said Audrey.

The actor who'd played Rudy turned to her. 'You didn't look anything up?'

'Such as?'

He sighed. 'So none of you thought to seek the Latin name of the blackthorn flower?'

Heads shaken all round.

'Perhaps you would have in time. But if none of you had got it by tomorrow lunch we would have propped the book up somewhere even more unmissable, open at the relevant page. Where is it now?'

'Middle landing windowsill,' said Honor. 'I'll go and get it.'

She started upstairs at a light trot, then seemed to remember the terrible thing that was supposed to have happened and slowed to a sorrowful trudge.

While Honor was gone we heard another siren, a different kind.

'Now what?' said Pete.

'That'll be the ambulance,' said Gerald Tozer.

'Ambulance?'

'For the body.' Gerald was sitting on an arm of one

of the couches now. He looked much more thoughtful than usual, almost like he believed this 'real murder' rubbish.

'Do we get to see old Rod with his head pulped?' Pete said hopefully.

'You certainly do not.' This was DCI Smurfit, Myrtle, as was, exiting the library. 'That's no sort of sight for an impressionable lad.'

'He's not impressionable,' said Angie.

'That's right,' said Pete. 'I can take it.'

'And probably relish it,' said Smurfit. 'Forget it. It's not going to happen.'

'I liked you better when you were a maid,' he said.

'And I would probably have liked you better when you were a babe in arms. Now I have to get a few things sorted here, but first I want this space cleared. You children, go into the dining room till the body's been removed.'

'We're not children,' said Angie.

'Can I tell them the Latin name of the flower first?' asked Honor, coming down the stairs flipping through the big old book.

'Dolly, this isn't a game any longer,' Smurfit said.

'It won't take a sec,' said Honor (or Dolly).

'Oh…all right. But be quick.'

The approaching siren stopped as Honor raised the

book to read from it. 'The Latin name of the blackthorn flower,' she said slowly, then paused and looked up. 'Anyone care to hazard a guess?'

'Just spit it out,' said my father irritably.

'The relaxation therapy's really working, isn't it?' Mum muttered.

Dad looked like he was going to snap at her, but the doorbell rang and he clamped his jaw instead.

'You three – dining room,' Smurfit said to us kids. 'Someone go with them to make sure they don't peek.'

'I'll go,' said Audrey.

'So will I,' said Mum.

'We're not leaving till we've heard the Latin clue,' said Pete.

'You want to hear *Latin*?' I asked him.

'Just this once, then it can go back to being a dead language.'

'Jane?' Honor asked.

Smurfit didn't look happy about the delay, but she gave a sharp little nod.

Honor cleared her throat. 'The Latin name of the blackthorn flower is...*Crataegus tomentosa*.'

While several puzzled eyes met other puzzled eyes, DCI Smurfit opened the door and spoke to the ambulance people outside.

'And that's the big clue?' Oliver said to Honor.

'An extremely generous clue,' said Rudy Bollinger, as was.

'Well, I don't get it.'

No one else did either.

'Let me see that,' Angie said, joining Honor and peering at the book in her hands.

'Before I let them in,' DCI Smurfit said from the door, 'I want everyone out of here, adults included. This isn't a spectator event.'

'Angie!' Audrey called as she and my mother steered me and Pete away and other Golden Oldies started to scatter.

'Aaaaah,' said Angie, still with Honor and the book.

'What?' I asked.

'You probably have to see it in print,' she said. 'Or hear the last two syllables emphasised.'

'Emphasised?'

'As in *Crataegus tomen*-tosa.' She looked at one of the people walking away. 'Yes?' she said to him.

Gerald stopped, chuckled, raised his hands. 'Got me bang to rights,' he said. 'Yes, it was I who shot Sir Duff, chucked Honor from the battlements, and drowned the butler.'

'Drowned the butler?' said Pete. 'You?'

'Me,' Gerald said cheerfully. 'And now that it's all

133

out in the open, I can admit that I was also...' — and here he switched to overcooked country-yokel-speak — '...Silas Blackthorrn, Naffington 'All garrrdener!'

CHAPTER THIRTEEN

'Tosa and Tozer,' I said when we were in the dining room with the door closed. 'Who would ever have guessed *that*?'

'I never even noticed the lousy book,' said Pete. 'Why would I? It's a *book*.'

'Got to hand it to Gerald, though,' Angie said. 'Sure had us fooled. And we never even *suspected* that he was also Blackthorn.'

'I bet you knew,' I said accusingly to my mother.

'Of course,' she said, looking away.

'And you?' Angie asked her mother.

Audrey shook her head. 'I'm just a guest, like you.'

'The Prossers,' I said to Mum. 'Guests or actors?'

'Oh, they're guests. Belinda really is Roderick's niece. This weekend was meant to be part of his wedding present to them.'

'Be a pretty memorable one if this was as on the up – and – up as you lot make out,' I said.

'On the up and up?' said Mum. 'Jig, we're not fooling now.'

'Oh, no, course you aren't. Since we got here all anyone's talked about is murder, and everyone who's been killed is out there now laughing and joking like nothing happened.'

'They're not laughing and joking.'

'No. They're trying to pull another fast one. But we're not buying it, are we?' I said to Pete and Angie.

They shook their heads like twin marionettes.

I turned back to my mother. 'But as we have to stay in here till they finish pretending to take Rod's bod away, why don't you tell us what Gerald's motive was supposed to be?'

'Motive?'

'For killing the first three.'

'It seems frivolous even to discuss that in the light of what's happened,' she said.

'Do it anyway,' I said.

She sighed. 'Gerald's character was Sir Duff's no-good younger brother who'd been abroad for so long that no one knew what he looked like now. The only people who stood in the way of his inheriting Naffington Hall and the family fortune were Sir Duff and his wife and daughter, so he decided to eliminate them. With Sir Duff and Honor disposed of, Lady Helga would have been next, but Bogart realised who Gerald was and what he'd done and threatened to turn him in, so Gerald drowned him in the lily pond.'

Audrey gave a weak, sad smile. 'Good old-fashioned murder mystery plotting.'

'Old-fashioned,' said Ange. 'I should say. Country houses, Sir this, Lady that, butlers, maids, libraries, dinner gongs...'

'People love such settings and characters,' said Mum.

'Not everyone,' said Pete.

'No,' I said. 'Maybe someone hated the material so much that he knocked off the bloke behind it.' I was joking, naturally. I still didn't believe a word of this.

'What if he's got a taste for it now?' Audrey said.

'Who, a taste for what?' Mum asked.

'The person who murdered Roderick. What if he fancies doing someone else in? If Roderick's killer's one of those people out there we could all be at risk. And we have a whole night to get through yet. I want to go home.'

'I don't think Jane will let us,' said Mum.

Audrey gasped. 'You mean we have to stay here with a killer in our midst?'

This was followed by a silence full of eyes that weren't sure where to look. I wanted to hold on to the smirk that would cover me when the whole thing was exposed as another murder weekend con. But there was this thing, this deep down thing, and this wormy little voice that squeaked, 'What if it's true? What if Mum and everyone else has suddenly turned *sincere*?' I glanced at Pete and Angie. Saw the same uncertainty on their phizogs. Then all three of us eye-contacted and suddenly we had no doubt, none at all, that there really had been a murder.

An actual murder.

That Roderick really had been carted away as a stiff.

That Myrtle the maid really was a detective chief inspector of police.

And suddenly we were scared, just like Audrey, just like my mother.

Really scared.

'It's starting to rain,' said Mum in a small, taut, I'm-changing-the-subject-to-take-my-mind-off-this sort of voice.

We all looked at the windows. Rain was hitting them. Running down the glass. Suddenly the rain was fascinating. It was all any of us wanted to look at or think about.

'Storm coming,' said Audrey when we heard distant thunder.

'Mm...'

Thunder. Even more fascinating than rain.

When the door opened suddenly we all span round as though expecting a raging bloodthirsty beast to bound in smacking its chops.

But it was just DCI Smurfit.

'You can come out now,' she said.

The only person still in the hall was Sergeant Fawkes, over by the phone. 'Line's dead,' he said as we went in.

Smurfit marched over to him. 'It was working when I phoned for the body squad.' She snatched the receiver, put it to her ear, jiggled the cradle, listened again. 'Brilliant,' she said, and hung up. 'And you can't get a mobile signal here for love or money. We need reinforcements, Sergeant. Armed backup. You'll have to radio from your car.'

'Yes, ma'am.'

'They really say "ma'am"?' Angie whispered. 'I thought that was telly talk.'

'It's usually "guv" on telly,' said Pete.

'She's not his guv,' I said. 'Just a higher ranking officer.'

Sergeant Fawkes went to the door and looked out. 'It's pouring,' he said.

'I'm sure you can make it to your car without catching cold,' said Smurfit.

He gave her a sour look and ran out with his arms over his head.

'Who's going to serve the food if you're not a maid any more?' Pete asked Smurfit.

She frowned. 'Food? You've not long eaten.'

'I might want something else. And there's breakfast tomorrow, and lunch.'

'I have other things to think about.' She turned to Mum and Audrey. 'Would you ladies care to join me in the library? I might as well start with you.'

'Start what?' Audrey asked.

'The interviews. I'll be talking to everyone in turn.'

'Just like the phoney inspector,' I said.

'Just like him,' Smurfit agreed, 'with one big difference. No one's acting now.'

'What about the kids?' Mum asked. 'We can't leave them on their own.'

'I don't run a crèche,' Smurfit snapped. 'Library!'

'You three,' Audrey said to us. 'Stick together and be very careful. It's no longer safe in this house.'

The library door closed behind the three of them. We were alone.

And nervous.

'So what do we do?' Pete said.

'If there's one thing I'm *not* going to do,' said Angie, 'it's cower down here.'

'What then?' I asked.

'I'm going to cower upstairs.'

As she headed for the stairs there was a deafening clap of thunder, followed by a blinding flash of light at the windows. Pete and I shoved her aside and belted past her. We beat her to our attic door by quite a way. When all three of us were on the other side of the door, we closed it, thinking that we'd lock it so no one could come up uninvited. Except...

'There's no key,' said Pete.

'Or bolt,' said Ange.

Crouching by the door wondering what to do next, I hoped I looked less vulnerable and scared than I felt. Probably not, though, because Angie said, 'Jig, you don't half look vulnerable and scared.'

We went up to the attic.

'What we need,' said Pete, 'is weapons.'

'Weapons?' I said.

'To defend ourselves if the murderer comes up.'

'There aren't any weapons here.'

Angie grabbed an ancient tennis racquet. 'There's this.'

'Well, let's hope he's in the mood for tennis,' I said.

'Marbles!' said Pete.

He pounced on the box of marbles he'd played with for about forty seconds the night before.

'Good plan,' said Angie. 'A game of marbles will definitely take our minds off the fact that our throats could be slit in our sleep.'

Pete went back down the stairs almost all the way, then sat on one and put some marbles on the step below – carefully so they wouldn't roll off – then backed up step by step, laying marbles on each one below him, till half the stairs were marbled.

'You know, that's quite a smart idea for a sparrow-brain,' Angie said when he rejoined us at the top.

'Thanks,' said Pete. 'That means a lot.'

We felt better knowing that anyone who tried to get up those stairs in the night would make such a clatter sliding around on the marbles that every non-murderer in the house would come running to our rescue.

While thunder roared and lightning made us flinch every few minutes, there could be only one topic of conversation now that we'd got our heads round what had happened.

'We should run through the possible suspects,' Angie said.

'We did that before,' said Pete. 'We got it wrong.'

'Yes, but that was a game, this isn't.'

'Which makes it even less likely that we'll guess who dun it.'

'It could be anyone,' I said.

'Except Roderick,' said Angie.

'And our parents,' said Pete.

'And the maid-turned-copper,' I said.

'Probably rule the Prossers out too,' said Ange.

'Why rule the Prossers out?' said Pete. 'If Belinda's Roderick's niece she could stand to inherit something if his head's bashed in, and Billy could get his hands on the inheritance through her.'

'OK, they're suspects too. Apart from them, listing the actors by the names of the characters they played, we have the inspector, Bogart, Lady Helga, Honor, Rudy Bollinger and Gerald Tozer. How many's that?'

'Six,' I said. 'Eight with the Prossers. Eight possible murderers.'

'My money's on the one who played the inspector and Sir Naff Duffington,' said Pete.

'Duff Naffington,' said Angie. 'Why him?'

'Why not?' said Pete.

'Cases aren't solved by people saying "Why not?"' Angie said.

'Why not?' Pete said again.

She clipped him round the ear.

'I bet it's Gerald again,' I said.

'Again?' said Ange.

'Yeah. He played the *part* of a murderer and wanted to find out what it feels like for real.'

143

'You don't think his former role makes him *too* likely a suspect?'

I shrugged. 'Maybe he didn't think of that in the heat of feeding Roderick's skull to the carpet.'

'Hang on,' said Pete. 'It can't be Gerald, or the Prossers. They were with us in the dining room when we heard Roderick had bought it.'

'They could have killed him before they went to dinner,' I said.

'Was one or more of them last in?' Angie asked.

We couldn't remember.

'What about Bogart?' said Pete. 'Last we saw of Roderick he was about to enter the room where Bogart was reading a magazine.'

'That's it!' I cried. 'He bludgeoned him to death with a magazine. Those staples, real killers.'

They ignored me.

'Bogart wasn't alone,' said Angie. 'Lady Helga was there too, smoking.'

'And as we know,' I said, 'smoking kills.'

They ignored me again.

'Bogart and Helga could have killed Roderick together,' Angie said. 'As a team.'

'If they did,' said Pete, 'they couldn't have done it there. Rod was found in the library. The library's on the ground floor and the actors' quarters aren't.'

144

Angie nodded. 'But there's a window next to their quarters. They might have shoved the corpse through it and carried him down to the library while no one was...' She stopped. Went all rigid. 'Listen!' Suddenly she was all ears.*

We listened. Heard the door at the bottom of the stairs opening. Swapped glances jammed solid with big eyes. Then Pete whispered, 'No worries, the marbles.' But now that the dreaded moment had come, marbles on stairs didn't seem such a terrific deterrent somehow. Pete and I only just managed not to bury our heads in one another's chests with our eyes shut, but Angie – typical Angie – went to the head of the stairs wielding her deadly tennis racquet and glared menacingly into the shadows below.

'Who's there?' she called – softly, like she hoped she wouldn't be heard. Maybe she wasn't, because there was no answer. All we heard was a creak, of a stair probably. 'Wh...who are you?' she asked next, in a trembly little voice.

This time there was an answer. Sort of. A deep, throaty chuckle.

'It's him!' Angie said, gaping down the stairs. 'The man in the hat!'

'The man in the hat?' I said from across the room.

---

* Well, not all ears exactly. She was also head, arms, legs and the rest of the girly stuff, but she was certainly paying attention to something.

'But he was Roderick – we think – and part of the murder weekend thing, not the real murderer.'

'All I know,' Angie said, 'is that there's a man in a hat at the bottom of our stairs, and he looks sinister. And there's one more thing.'

'What's that?'

'He's coming up.'

That did it. Suddenly we were Action Kids. Pete's action was to jump up, run into the toilet and slam the door. Mine and Angie's was to flee to the only other door, fling it open, and run out onto the rain-soaked roof. Angie dropped the lethal tennis racquet on the way.

CHAPTER FOURTEEN

Out on the roof Angie and I huddled under a stretch of overhang so as not to get any wetter than we had to. 'If you could design the weather for a murder weekend,' she said, 'you'd absolutely go for this. Still, at least the thunder and lightning's stopped.'

'Ange,' I said. 'There's a hat-wearing murderer on our heels.'

'I know. That's why we're out here.'

'A murderer on our heels and you're talking about the *weather*?'

'It helps take my mind off him. And Pete.'

'Pete?'

'He's at the man in the hat's mercy.'

'Only if the man in the hat goes into the toilet.'

'He could. There's no bolt on the door. He could just walk in and do his worst.'

'What, have a pee without asking Pete to leave first?'

'I mean kill him.'

'Did you see his face?'

'Yes. He looked terrified.'

'The man in the hat looked terrified?'

'I mean Pete.'

'So you didn't see the man in the hat's face on the stairs?'

'No, he kept the brim down.'

'Could he have been Bogart?'

'He could have been anybody.'

'Even Lady Helga?'

'Any *man*. And maybe we shouldn't hang about in case he comes after us.'

'Absolutely,' I said. 'Any thoughts?'

'Thoughts?'

'Like where we should go apart from over the battlements to our screaming deaths like Honor Naffington.'

'I have a very good thought,' she said, covering her hair to keep the rain off and running to the door in the side of the tower and tugging it open.

'Yeah, that beats the battlement route,' I said.

I went after her, not covering my hair, shot into the tower and closed the door firmly. It was dark in there. Very dark.

'Where are you?' I asked.

'Here.'

'How do I know that's you?'

'By my voice, you pillock.'

'You might be a female impersonator.'

'Well, I'm not,' she said. 'Which way? Up or down?'

'You decide.'

'Why do I always have to make all the decisions?'

'Because you're so good at them.'

'All right. Up. We don't want to go down to the house in case he does too.'

'What if he follows us?'

'He won't be able to if we bolt the door.'

'I can't find the door,' I said.

'It's just there.'

'Ow!'

'What did I just hit?' she asked

'My groinal region.'

'Well, keep it to yourself.'

'I was trying to. How was I to know you were going to—'

'Quiet!'

'Quiet?' I said. 'Why?'

'I think I hear movement out on the roof.'

I listened. 'I can't hear anything.'

'Well, I did. I think.'

'You might have imagined it.'

'And I might not.'

'You think it's him?'

'I don't know, but I'm not opening the door to ask. Follow me!'

'Follow you? How, if I can't see you?'

'McCue, have I ever told you what a useless specimen you are? Take my hand!'

'Your what?'

'My hand, my hand! What is it, a new word for you?'

'Angie, we haven't held hands since we were a year and a half.'

'You're right,' she said, grabbing one of my elbows and lugging it.

'How come you can see and I can't?' I asked as we set off.

'I'm a girl.'

'Oh. Right.' There are lots of things I don't get about girls. Super sight is a new one, but maybe it's part of the apparatus.

A few steps later we stopped, and Angie said, 'Change of plan. We're going down.'

'Down?'

'Yes. If we go up and he comes after us we'll be trapped, nowhere to go. You first.'

'Me first?' I said, hoping my voice didn't suddenly sound too high. 'Why me first?'

'I'm trying to develop your leadership skills.'

'Oh, thanks, I appreciate that.'

We started groping our way slowly-slowly down the inside of the dark-dark tower, me first, feeling each step as it came, toe by toe, heel by heel, quiet as mice in bedsocks. It wasn't easy not to imagine the man in the hat following us, just as quietly, with a hammer or heavy candlestick or something.

'Of course,' Angie said as we descended, 'if Lady Helga and Bogart are in cahoots, one of them could be coming up from below right this minute.'

I stopped. Abruptly. She crashed into my shoulders from behind.

'What did you stop for?' she demanded.

'Hey, I don't know,' I said, stroking my chin in the dark. 'Maybe it was the thought of a second murderer waiting for me round the very next bend.'

'Yes, but the man in the hat's up above, so it would only be Lady Helga.'

'She might have a chainsaw.'

'Get down there, you lily-livered worm,' Angie said. 'And stop talking.'

'Stop talking?' I said. 'Talking helps in tense situations, haven't you heard?'

'It also tells men in hats where people are.'

'And actresses with hatchets.'

'I thought it was a chainsaw?'

'It might not be easy to tell the difference in the dark before my head comes off.'

'Chainsaws are noisier. If you hear a chainsaw you ought to duck.'

'I'll try and remember that.'

'Good. Now zip those lips.'

We carried on down. And down. Slowly. Round and round and round. The only time we could see how we were doing was when there was a flash of white light at one of the little windows.

'The lightning hasn't stopped,' I said.

'Shut up,' said Angie.

There was a roar of thunder. 'Thunder either,' I said.

After that I kept quiet. But it was a tall tower, and after a while the silence got hard to bear, so I thought I'd risk a whisper.

'Angie...'

No answer.

'Ange?'

Still no answer.

I stopped. This time she didn't crash into my shoulders.

I turned.

Groped the dark.

Felt no one.

'Ange?'

A third answer of the zero variety. Which left me with a pair of those sickening choices that keep popping up in my life like sitting ducks at a fairground: to carry on descending at a sudden Olympic trot hoping not to bump into any middle-aged hatchet- or chainsaw-wielding actresses, or creep back up and see what had happened to Angie. The second of these wasn't much more appealing than the first, to be honest. I mean, suppose the man in the hat – Bogart, if it was him – had got her and was waiting for me to go and check on her? But up I went, and after a couple of twists of the stairs I found her. She hadn't been pulped or gutted or any of the other things murderers do to innocent victims for fun. She was standing by one of the little windows.

'What are you doing?'

'Listening to the thunder, watching the lightning. Weird lightning. Can't see where it's coming from.'

'My guess is the sky,' I said. 'Couldn't you have mentioned that you were going to stop on the way down?'

'It was an impulse.'

'Impulse. OK. Well, when you're all impulsed out...'

We carried on down to the bottom of the tower and opened the door to the games room – carefully, begging it not to creak.

It creaked.

We pulled the curtain aside. The room was in darkness, but the door to the hall was open a fraction and the chandelier out there was on, all 463 bulbs blazing.

'What now?' Angie said.

'How about finding some big Golden Oldies to hide behind?'

'We'd better tell DCI whatever-her-name-is –'

'Smurfit.'

'– about the man in the hat being upstairs. He could be carving Pete into small pieces in the toilet as we speak.'

'That's something I don't want to think about,' I said.

'Pete being carved up?'

'Pete in the toilet.'

There was no one in the hall until we went into it, but as we were standing there wondering where to go next, DCI Smurfit came in the front door.

'You look worried,' Angie said to her. 'And wet.'

'Sergeant Fawkes has disappeared,' said Smurfit.

'Disappeared?'

'He's not out there. His car's there, but he's not.'

'Maybe he went for a stroll,' I said.

'In this weather? Don't be silly. Why are you two

hanging around here when there's a killer in our midst?'

'Glad you mention that,' Angie said. 'The thing is—'

'Never mind. I'm going to call for backup on the sergeant's radio and I want you to wait here. *Right* here. Is that understood? Do. Not. Move.'

She went back out, closing the door after her.

'Who does she think she is, giving us orders?' Angie said.

'Probably a detective chief inspector of police,' I said.

'What's going on?' said a sudden voice.

We turned. My dad, peering round the dining room door.

'The sergeant's disappeared,' said Angie.

'There's never a cop around when you want one,' said Dad.

'What are you doing in there?' I asked.

'Feasting off scraps with Ollie.'

'How can you eat at a time like this?'

'We missed a meal.' He closed the door.

And another opened. The front door. Smurfit again, wetter than ever.

'The wires have been yanked,' she said.

'Wires?' I said. 'What wires?'

'The sergeant's radio's. You know what this means?

155

Someone's put him out of action. The same person who cut the landline, no doubt. In light of which, I think this door had better be...'

She slammed it, turned the key and was about to ram the two big bolts home when Angie leaped forward.

'Don't! We might need to escape!'

Smurfit hesitated. 'Escape?'

'The murderer's not out there, he's in here.'

'You've seen him?'

'Well, we've seen a man in a hat.'

'A man in a hat?'

'Yes. We think he's the one who killed Roderick. And don't ask us who he is because we don't know – the brim was pulled down.'

'When did you see him?'

'Ten minutes ago, fifteen. Upstairs.'

'I'd better go and see if I can find him then.'

'He might leap out and massacre you,' I cautioned.

She smiled grimly. 'I can handle myself.'

'That's what they all say before they're found slumped in corners or hanging from beams.'

'That's in fiction and films. And I'm trained in unarmed combat.'

'He might not be unarmed.'

'Let me worry about that. Where's the other boy?'

'Pete? He's in the toilet.'

'Best place in the circumstances. You two stay put till I return.'

As Smurfit went upstairs, Angie whispered, 'Give her a minute. If she doesn't come down we'll go up.'

'Why, so the murderer can roll us around in her blood while chuckling fiendishly?'

'To check on Pete. I want to be sure he's still in one piece.'

'Can't we just *trust* that he is?' I suggested.

'You trust. Me, I need to see that piece with my own eyes.'

We waited a minute – she timed it – then Angie said, 'Right,' and marched to an umbrella stand by the front door and pulled out a heavy walking stick. 'You'd better arm yourself too,' she said, heading for the stairs holding the walking stick out in front of her.

I trotted to the umbrella stand, tugged the first handle I gripped and went after her in a hurry. I was halfway up the stairs before I realised that I was holding a Little Pink Pony umbrella.

Up on the landing we found all the doors closed and no sign of Smurfit.

'Where'd you think she went?' I wondered.

'Hang on, I'll ring and ask her,' Angie said. 'Oh, wait, problem with that.'

'There's no need to be sarcastic,' I said.

'No, but I enjoy it,' she said.

We went to the door to our attic. Also closed.

'Was it shut before?' I asked.

'Not when I last saw it. The man in the hat had just opened it.'

'Maybe he closed it before going down to strangle the sergeant and yank the wires out of his radio.'

'Maybe. Or before going up and butchering Pete in the toilet.'

'If he did that he might still be up there,' I said.

'Yes. That's why one of us is carrying a sensible weapon.'

She opened the door, super quietly, and we stood looking up the stairs into very deep shadows.

'The lights were on when we went onto the roof,' I said. 'They're not now.'

'No,' said Ange.

'So what do you say we discuss our next move downstairs, with people we know and would respect if they weren't our parents?'

'No,' she said, far too firmly for my liking. 'We're going up.'

'After you,' I said.

'Together,' she said, again far too firmly.

She clamped one of my hips to one of hers and, holding our heavy walking stick and Little Pink

Pony umbrella in front of us, we started up like we were glued together. We'd gone about six steps when we remembered the marbles Pete had laid down. We remembered them because our feet suddenly slid backwards and we dropped to our knees and clunked down stair by stair on our tummy-tum-tums and chesty-chest-chests, going something like, 'Uh-uh-uh-uh-uh-uh-uh-uh-uh,' all the way.

We'd just about reached the bottom when a terrifying figure leaped out of the darkness above, also slipped on the marbles, and landed on top of us while trying to beat us to death with a deadly weapon.

159

CHAPTER FIFTEEN

The deadly weapon turned out to be the clockwork train set's signal box. And the terrifying figure? Pete. The signal box had been the first thing that fell into his hands before he threw himself down the stairs at us.

'I thought you were him,' he said once Ange and I had stopped calling him names that would have got us suspended from school.

'You might have *asked*,' said Angie, patting her hair.

'Did you see him?' I asked, not patting mine.

'Who?'

'The man in the hat.'

'No. I was in the toilet.'

'He didn't come in after you then?'

'No. Must've realised it was engaged. I thought he was outside all this time keeping quiet and still. Didn't hear a sound till just now when I decided to act.'

'By attacking us with a toy signal box.'

'How was I to know it was you? Thanks for abandoning me, by the way. Do the same for you some time.'

'No one forced you into the toilet,' I said.

'Well, now that we know he's not up there and Pete's still in that one piece of his,' Angie said, 'we'd better go down again.'

'What for?' Pete asked.

'To be with other people. Also because Smurfit said we had to stay there.'

'She didn't say it to me.'

'Only because you weren't there. One thing to remember,' she said as she led the way down. 'None of us must be alone with someone who isn't another of us because anyone except our parents might be the murderer.'

'*Anyone.*'

Down in the hall we found two men standing by the fireplace – the actors who'd played Gerald Tozer and Inspector Qwerty. I didn't know Gerald's real name, but I'll call the other one Reg Mote from now on. Can't keep calling him the inspector when he wasn't one.

'Hello, hello, hatching another dastardly plot, are we?' Angie said.

'Things are on an altogether different level now,' said Reg Mote.

'I hope you're still taking notes,' I said to Gerald.

'The note-taking was part of the subterfuge,' he said. 'All I want now is to get away from here.'

'Because you killed Roderick?' said Pete.

'Me? You're kidding. No, because there might be another victim, and it could be me.'

'How do you know he isn't the killer?' Angie said, nodding towards Reg.

Reg's mouth dropped open in surprise. 'Me?'

'It's no good looking like that,' she said. 'Expressions and false identities are what you do.' She glared at Gerald. 'Both of you.'

'I can't blame you for suspecting us,' said Gerald, 'but Reg and I have known one another for years. We'd trust each other with our lives.'

'I wouldn't go that far,' said Reg. He said it seriously, but Gerald laughed. The laugh lightened things up a bit.

'I can see it now,' Angie said to Gerald.

'See what?'

'The likeness to Blackthorn the gardener.'

He grinned. 'Good disguise, wasn't it?'

'Total cliché,' said Ange.

'Blackthorn was meant to be a cliché. It was hoped that one or more of you guests would see through him, suspect him and thus be thrown off track.'

'We did, we did, we were. But a flower book with part of the character's name in *Latin*? You might want to rethink that for your murder weekends.'

'No chance of those now,' said Reg sadly. 'Roderick was the brains behind them. The organiser. Without him there's no future of any kind for The Pure Isle Players.'

'Have either of you got a hat?' I asked in the silence that followed this.

'Hat?' said Gerald. 'What sort of hat?'

'One with a brim.'

'The only brimmed hat I have is my trilby. It's in our quarters with the other Pure Isle accoutrements. Why d'you ask?'

'We think the murderer's a hat-wearer.'

'And because we don't know who he is yet' Angie said, 'the three of us are staying right here, together. No chance of being snuck up on under a chandelier as bright as that.'

The chandelier went out.

Every last bright bulb of it.

'Did you really have to say that?' I asked in the sudden total darkness.

It really was total too, because every other light in the house had snuffed it at the very same moment. Others noticed this, starting with DCI Smurfit somewhere upstairs.

'Who turned the lights off?' she shouted down.

'Not us!' Angie shouted back.

Then Oliver, from the dining room. 'Who turned the lights off?'

'Not us!' I shouted.

Then Belinda Prosser, from Billy's and her room off the landing. 'Who turned the lights off?'

'Not us!' shouted Gerald Tozer.

Then the Honor Naffington actress from somewhere else. 'Who turned the lights off?'

'Oh, give it a rest!' shouted Pete.

In the darkness we could just make out shadowy figures feeling their way downstairs and out of nearby rooms.

'I don't like this,' Angie whispered.

'Good to know,' I whispered back. 'Hate to think I was the only one who enjoyed total darkness with a mad killer on the loose.'

'Any one of them could be looking for his or her next victim and we wouldn't see who killed us,' said Ange.

'We might not care after it's done,' said Pete.

'Whose arm am I gripping?' Angie asked.

'If you're the gripper,' I said, 'it's mine.'

'OK. Pete?'

'What?'

'That your arm?'

'No.'

'Well, I'm gripping someone's.'

'Mine,' I said. 'I told you.'

'Someone else's too.'

'It's mine,' Pete admitted.

'You said it wasn't,' Angie said.

'I was joking.'

'Joking? At a time like this? Now listen. Both of you. If you feel me ungrip, make a run for it because I'll have been got.'

'If we ran in this darkness we'd probably fall over something,' I said.

'So run carefully. Now shut the hell up.'

With this she tugged our biceps away from the fireplace.

'Angie?' Audrey's voice in the darkness.

'Pete?' Oliver's voice.

'Jiggy?' My mother's voice.

'Don't answer.' Angie's voice.

'But they're not the murderers.' My voice.

'No, but we don't want to give away our location to the *actual* murderer, do we?'

She shoved us into a room we'd come to and closed the door behind us. It was a moonless night but just enough light leaked in the window at the far end to tell us that we were back in the games room.

'Lock the door,' Angie said.

'I'm trying to,' said Pete. 'Seems to be another one without a key.'

'If we can't lock the door,' I said, 'anyone could come in, including the murderer.'

'What happened to the lights?' said a voice in the darkness behind us.

We span round. At least I did. I think the others did too, but I couldn't see them.

'Who's that?' gasped a small voice amazingly like mine.

'Billy Prosser. The lights?'

A dark shape rose from a chair across the room and became a menacing silhouette against the pathetic light coming from the window.

'They went off,' Angie said. 'What are you doing here?'

The menacing silhouette headed our way. 'I was reading some work stuff.'

'Work stuff? Alone?'

'Alone is best when you're trying to concentrate. I started a new job just before Belinda and I got married. Bit too demanding for my liking – the job, not married life – but you take what you can get these days.'

'Don't you know there's a killer in the house?'

Angie said. 'He could have strolled in and garrotted you while you were reading.'

'I'd have seen him coming from where I was sitting,' said Billy.

'How do we know you're not the murderer?' Pete asked.

'You still suspect me?' said Billy, very close to us now.

'We suspect everyone,' Angie said, grabbing Billy by the arm, opening the door and throwing him into the hall. 'Lean against the door!' she ordered, slamming it.

Pete and I flattened a shoulder each against the door, and so did Angie, which made it kind of crowded. Three separate doors would have given us more room, but one of our shoulders per door wouldn't have kept a kitten out.

'How long do we have to stay like this?' Pete asked after a time or two.

'Long as it takes,' said Ange.

'That could be all night.'

'It could. Unless we put something else against it.'

'Like what?'

'Something heavy. Such as the pool table.'

'The pool table?' I said. 'You mean drag it over here?'

'Well, it won't come if you whistle for it.'

'If we leave the door to get the pool table the murderer might charge in waving a weapon.'

'He might also charge in waving a toffee apple,' Angie said, 'but we'll have to chance that. Come on!'

We raced through the dark towards the pool table. One of us raced inaccurately, and swore when part of him connected with the corner of the table. When Pete had recovered we dragged the table to the door and lodged it end-on so the murderer would have more table to push. It was when we were as sure as could be that only a very strong man in a hat would be able to get in, that I had one of those thoughts that you can do without at times like that.

'How do we know we haven't blocked the door to stop anyone coming in and rescuing us?' I asked.

'Rescuing us from what?' said Angie.

'The killer in the room.'

'Killer in the room? The only person here was Billy Prosser and I kicked him out.'

'You did. But we couldn't see Billy sitting over there in the dark, so how do we know there isn't someone else in here that we also can't see?'

'Billy said he was alone.'

'He might not have known he wasn't. Don't forget the curtain over the door to the tower.'

'You think someone could be curtain-lurking?'

'Might be.'

'Well, we'd better find out.' She turned to face the curtain – from a distance. 'Is there anyone behind the curtain?' she asked.

No one answered.

'Good,' said Ange. 'We're alone.'

'Unless he's keeping quiet,' said Pete.

'Mm,' said Ange. She started feeling her way across the room.

'Where you going?' I asked.

'The curtain.'

'He might be standing quietly behind it getting ready to pounce on you.'

'Yes…'

She swerved and I could just make out her dim dark figure feeling its way to the rack that held the pool cues. She took a cue down and went to the curtain, which she prodded with the cue.

'Come out,' she said. 'We know you're in there.'

'Do we?' said Pete in a suddenly high voice.

'She's calling his bluff,' I whispered. 'Well, she is if he's there.'

'OK, if that's how you want to play it…' Angie said.

Pete and I grabbed hold of one another. There are times when a kid needs someone big and strong to hold on to. Pity we only had each other.

Angie jerked the curtain aside, all set to strike with the cue if there was anyone there. There wasn't. Pete and I put each other down before she could notice our shadowy figures embracing and ask when we were moving in together.

CHAPTER SIXTEEN

To pass the time we tried playing pool, but it wasn't easy in the dark, and besides, with one end of the pool table against the door there were only three clear angles. We tried darts too, but as we could hardly make out the board, the wall got more bullseyes. A game of cards also wasn't as much fun as it might have been if we'd been able to see what was on the cards, but at least we were able to cheat.

'Where are we going to sleep?' I wondered when we were so bored that we were close to dropping off. 'I don't fancy making a dash up the tower in the dark with an unknown killer about.'

'Oh, so you'd be all right with it if the killer was known,' said Pete.

'We'll have to sleep here,' said Angie.

'This is a games room,' I said. 'No beds.'

'There's a sort of couch next to the cue rack.'

'It's very narrow. Like a church pew with a cushion. You'd have to lie sideways to stay on it.'

'I can do that,' said Ange.

'I think we ought to toss for it,' I said.

'No point. We wouldn't be able to tell heads from tails. No, I'll take it, save argument.'

'I'm going on this,' said Pete, dragging what seemed to be a sheepskin rug across to the pool table and spreading it out beneath it.

'So what does that leave for me?' I said.

'There's the armchair by the window,' said Ange.

'But I'd have to sleep sitting up.'

'Ah, stop whingeing, McCue!'

So I slept in the armchair. Some of the night anyway. It wasn't an easy chair to snooze in, but I must have dozed eventually because something woke me. The sound of a nearby window opening. My eyes also opened, kind of nervously. In the dim light from outside, I saw a hulking figure standing next to me. Then there was this fierce whooshing sound like water from a hosepipe hitting the bushes outside. Then the hulking shape closed the window again.

'Whew, I needed that,' his voice said.

'Pete?' I said.

'Yeah.'

'What were you doing?'

'Taking a leak out of the window.'

'But I was sitting right next to it!'

'So? I've stood next to you all our lives while peeing.'

172

'Not usually out of a window.'

'It was all there was. God, you're turning into your mother, the way you go on sometimes.'

'There's no running water,' said Angie from the pew by the cue rack.

'There was just now,' said Pete.

'I mean to wash your hands.'

'So what am I supposed to do, leave the room and get chopped to pieces by the mad axeman?'

'He might not have an axe. He might just garrotte you.'

'Yeah, well, if it's all the same to you I'll give the hand-washing a miss.'

'Just make sure you don't touch me then,' Angie said.

'I wasn't planning to.'

We all took another snooze break.

Until I heard the window opening again.

'Garrett!' I said, eyes still shut. 'Get back under that pool table!'

He didn't answer, so I flipped the McCue orbs ajar. Pete wasn't there, but the window was still opening, slowly. I shifted my position to look through the glass. There was someone outside.

A man in a hat.

I shot out of the chair, raced across the room,

skidded on the floor, and crashed into a card table, which collapsed.

'What now?' snarled Angie from her pew next to the cues.

'There's someone at the window! A man! In a hat! Trying to get in!'

'There isn't,' she said, looking that way.

'There is, there is!'

'So he's invisible, is he?'

I separated myself from the ruins of the card table. 'He was there, I tell you.'

'You were dreaming,' said Angie.

I returned to the window. 'If I was dreaming, how come this is open?'

'Pete can't have closed it properly.'

'I did,' said Pete sleepily. 'I think.'

'Well, this time *I'll* do it.' Angie leaped off the pew, fell over something, got up, and cursed her way to the window. 'Definitely open,' she said, inspecting it.

'Must have been the wind,' mumbled Pete.

'It doesn't look windy out.' Angie closed the window. 'Now do you two mind if I get some more shuteye? I need my beauty sleep.'

'You do,' I agreed, sinking back into my chair.

We went quiet again.

Time passed.

Until I heard this suspicious shushing sound over by the door.

The McCue lids sprang up once more.

'Ange!' I hissed.

No answer.

'Pete!' I hissed.

'Zzzzz-zzz-zzzz.'

I sat there listening to the silence, the snoring and the shushing, staring at the door, which was opening, fraction by fraction, pushing the pool table back, centimetre by centimetre. The shushing was the table's legs moving slowly across the carpet. At last I leaped into action, ran to Angie's pew, gripped her shoulder.

'Aaaagh!'

That was her.

Then raced to the pool table and kicked Pete.

'Gerroff!'

That was him.

They were still stirring themselves when I put all my strength against the end of the pool table.

'I need help here!' I said.

Then all three of us were leaning against the table trying to stop the door opening further.

'Who's there?' Angie asked the widening black gap in the door.

All that came back was a throaty chuckle. The same

throaty chuckle we'd heard earlier, at the foot of the attic stairs.

We pushed harder, but the man in the hat (it had to be him) was stronger than us and the door kept on pushing the pool table back, and us with it, bit by tiny bit. Another half-minute at this rate and he would be in, and...

'Help!' shouted Pete.

'Who are you shouting for?' I asked.

'Anyone, not fussy. Help! Help!'

The throaty chuckle on the other side of the door came again.

'The cry for help doesn't seem to worry him,' said Angie.

'There's probably no one left *to* help us,' I said.

'Well, this is it,' said Pete. 'We've had our chips.'

'There's more to life than chips, Garrett,' I said.

'Not a lot,' he said. 'I wish I was in a chip shop now.'

'Middle of the night. You wouldn't find one open.'

'No, but I wish I was in one.'

'Shut up, you two,' said Angie. 'Put your backs into it, not your mouths.'

We put our backs into it, but the door kept on coming, and so did the pool table, and I began to get nervous. Did I say *began*? I was almost crossing my legs, which isn't easy when you're trying to put all your weight against a pool table to stop a man in a hat coming in.

'If ever there was a "one for all and all for lunch" moment,' I said, 'this is it.'

'Are we really still doing that?' said Angie.

'Doing what?'

'"One for all and all for lunch."'

'Why wouldn't we be?'

'Well, because…let me see…we're growing up?'

'Speak for yourself,' I said.

'She's right,' said Pete. 'Time we ditched all that kiddie crap.'

I gaped at him in the dark. 'You mean stop using our "One for all and all for lunch" rallying cry?'

'I mean the whole Musketeer thing. It's been a drag for a while now.'

'It was OK when we were young,' said Angie. 'But teenagers calling themselves The Three Musketeers? If it ever gets onto Facebook I'm done for. Exam and murder stress will be nothing compared to *that* fallout!'

I couldn't believe I was hearing this. 'I can't believe I'm hearing this,' I said.

'Well you are, so get over it.'

'But all the stuff the Musketeers have been through together: psychotic Y-fronts, body swaps, snot-eating creatures from council tips, clothes disappearing in public, kid-gulping giant slugs, devils the size of—'*

'Stop!' Angie said, holding her hand up. 'This is not the time for dewy-eyed reminiscences. A murderer's trying to get at us, and if we want to see another day, we have some serious pushing to do.'

'I don't think we do,' said Pete.

'What?'

'The table's stopped moving. So's the door.'

We looked. He was right. Angie raised her voice.

'Hey, man in a hat! You still there?'

No reply. Not even a throaty chuckle.

'Right,' she said next. 'Here's our chance. Push! Hard! '

We pushed the table, hard, and it moved forward, the door closed, and we leaned there, triumphant.

'He probably knew he didn't stand a chance against us,' said Pete.

'Or someone was coming,' said Ange.

'If someone was coming,' I said, 'it means he hasn't killed everyone.'

'No. Right. So...' She took a big breath. 'Help! Help!'

No one answered, no one came. The house stayed silent and still.

'They could have locked themselves in their rooms,' I said.

---

* See *The Killer Underpants*, *The Toilet of Doom*, *The Snottle*, *Nudie Dudie*, *Ryan's Brain*, *Neville the Devil* (not to mention the insane adventures in the other Jiggy McCue books).

'Even the ones who should be worried sick about their kids and prepared to risk their lives for them?' said Angie.

'Even those. Maybe the smart move would be to put something against the table in case the man in the hat has another shot at getting in.'

'Something like what?'

I looked around the dim room. 'The armchair?'

'Not heavy enough to make much difference. A couple of dead weights on the table might do it, though.'

'Dead weights?'

'You and Pete.'

'Us? On the table?'

'Yes. Get up there.'

'Why us? Why not you?'

'Because you're boys.'

'Oh, you say that when it suits you.'

'Yes. Go on, up.'

'It might not take the weight of both of us.'

'There's only one way to find out. Up!'

Pete clambered onto the pool table and stretched out.

'Not very comfortable,' he said.

'It's a table,' said Ange. 'Now you,' she said to me.

I joined Pete on the table. It didn't collapse.

'Now go to sleep,' Angie said.

'Sleep?' I said. 'On this?'

'Take it or leave it.'

'Thanks, I'll leave it.' I started to get off.

'Stay!' she commanded, like I was a dog.

I stayed. She went to the chair I'd been dozing in and curled up in it, all nice and neat. How do girls do that? When I try curling up in chairs nothing of me fits, but when girls do it, it's like the chairs are built round them. Anyway, Pete was soon snoring even though he was sleeping on baize-covered wood, and even I must have snoozed again after a while, because one minute it was dark and the next it wasn't. We might have slept longer if not for a sudden bang out in the hall.

'What was that?' said Angie, from the knees she'd fallen to in front of the armchair she'd just jerked out of in shock.

'It was a sudden bang,' I informed her. 'Out in the hall.'

'A gunshot?'

'Could've been a balloon.'

'What'd it sound like to you, Pete?' she asked, getting up from her knees.

'Zzzzz-zzz-zzzz,' said Pete, next to me on the table.

I lifted his arm off me and climbed off the pool table. Angie came over and shook him. 'Wake up, Garrett, you've been shot.'

He opened a bleary eye, then closed it, turned over, carried on snoring.

'What do we do?' Angie said.

'We could prod him with a pool cue.'

'I mean about the gunshot.'

'It *might* have been a balloon,' I said.

'And it might not. So what do we do?'

'Um…'

Before I could come up with a really terrific plan we heard a scream from the other side of the door.

'That sounded like my mum,' Angie said.

'It could've been anyone,' I said. 'Though probably not a man.'

'No, it was definitely my—'

Another scream cut her words off in their prime.

'That wasn't your mum,' I said.

'Or a man,' she said. 'Something's happening out there.'

'Maybe they're just holding scream practice. You know, the murder weekend version of choir practice.'

'Let's get this door open.'

'Is that wise?' I said.

'There are people out there screaming,' she said.

'Yes. Out there. There's no one in here doing it, so why not let them get on with it?'

But she'd stopped harking to my words of wisdom.

'Garrett,' she said, rapping the back of his head with her knuckles. 'Off this table! Now!'

Pete rolled over and opened his eyes. He looked like he was about to say something, but Angie grabbed his arm and pulled it towards her, which meant the rest of him felt sort of obliged to follow. Angie started pulling the table back while he was still getting up from the floor.

'Jig!'

Which meant I had to help.

'Pete!'

Him too. So the three of us pulled the table we'd so carefully pushed just a few hours earlier, pulled and pulled and pulled, until there was enough space to open the door and for one of us to get through the gap.

'Ladies first,' I said. I'm very old-fashioned about things like that.

Angie went out into the hall.

Pete and I waited for a minute.

'Oh-my-God, oh-my-God!'

Angie's voice.

We slipped out. Audrey and my mum were there, and the Prossers, and all four of them, plus Angie, were standing around one of the high-backed armchairs by the fireplace.

'There you are,' said Mum, seeing me.

'And there you are,' I said. 'Where have you been all night?'

'Upstairs, locked in with your dad.'

'And you didn't wonder if I was all right?'

'We saw the three of you go into the games room. Knew you'd be all right if you stuck together.'

'Why, because we're so good at martial arts and can deflect speeding bullets with our palms?'

'Speaking of bullets...' Angie said.

She beckoned to us. Pointed at the chair they were standing by.

'I don't think you should see this,' Mum said to Pete and me.

'Angie has,' said Pete.

'Yes, but she's a girl. Girls are made of stronger stuff.'

We flexed our chests and stormed to the chair.

And saw what all the screaming and oh-my-Godding had been about. Detective Chief Inspector Smurfit sat in the chair with her eyes closed. There was a small, perfect hole in her forehead.

The hole was red.

And dribbling.

CHAPTER SEVENTEEN

I used most of the pause that followed the sight of Smurfit's dribbling head-hole to glance around for a burst balloon. I couldn't see one, so I gulped and transferred the glance to Pete. Saw him gulping too.

'Were any of you here when this happened?' Angie asked as the pause dived slowly into the rug.

'I think we all came down together, didn't we?' Belinda Prosser said to the others.

They nodded or muttered yesses or *mmms*. Angie asked where the dads were and my mother said they'd gone for a stroll in the grounds.

'Before or after the gunshot?'

'Oh, before, definitely before.'

Just then the front door opened and several people spilled in at once – the actors: Gerald Tozer, Larry Bogart, Lady Helga, Honor, Rudy, Reg Mote.

'We thought we heard a bang,' one of them said.

'You did,' said Billy Prosser.

He nodded towards the chair. The actors went to it.

'My God!'

'Holy crap!'

'Squawk!'

'Who could have done this?' said Larry Bogart.

'Obviously the person who killed my dad,' said Rudy Bollinger.

'Oh, *really*?' said Gerald sarcastically.

'Where were you lot when the shot was fired?' Angie asked the actors.

'On our way here,' said the one who'd played Honor Naffington.

'All of you? Together?'

Honor glanced at the others, like she thought there might be something to hide. 'Well, not all from the same *direction...*'

'So any one of you could have done this,' Angie said.

Three voices blurted, 'It wasn't *me*,' but suddenly people who'd been standing together shuffled away from one another like they half expected the person next to them to stick something sharp in their ribs.

'Let's get out of here,' I whispered to Pete and Angie.

'We haven't had breakfast yet,' said Pete.

'You have an appetite with a second real dead body on the premises?' Angie said.

'Sure, why wouldn't I?'

'Well, put it on hold.' She gripped his arm and walked it to the door.

'Where are you three going?' Mum asked as we headed out.

'Lung or two of air,' I told her.

'You should stay here. There's a murderer about.'

'Yep,' I said. 'Look around, take your pick.'

When the door was shut behind us, Pete said, 'And we've left because…?'

'Because,' I said, 'being in a room with a bullet-ridden corpse makes me nervous.'

'One bullet isn't bullet-*ridden*.'

'It's still one too many when we know that one of those people in there's the one that holed Smurfit.'

'Unless someone else is involved,' Angie said. 'Someone we haven't met.'

'You mean another actor?' I said.

'Not necessarily. Just someone who kills people.'

'*Just* someone who kills people? You make it sound like a hobby.'

'Maybe it is. Maybe he used to collect seaside postcards and got bored.'

'Well, I still reckon it's one of the actors.'

'Look – the dads,' said Pete.

They were sitting on a bench near the gardener's

potting shed. The shed was open and Dad was gripping a rake like it was a spear and Oliver was trying to decapitate passing insects with the old garden shears, the ones with the pointy ends of the blades snapped off.

'What are you doing out here?' Angie asked them.

'Avoiding the luvvies,' said Oliver.

'You came out before they came in.'

'We came out because we expected them any time. Had all we can take of that mob, haven't we, Mel?'

'Too right,' said Dad.

'Your wife's a luvvie,' I reminded him.

'Yeah, she always did over-dramatise things,' he muttered.

'She's not over-dramatising now. None of them are. It's real now.'

'If you mean Roderick,' said Dad, 'I didn't take to him anyway.'

'I don't just mean Roderick.'

'What then?'

'Oh, of course,' said Angie. 'You two don't know about Smurfit.'

'We know all we need to about that one,' said Ollie.

'There's something else now,' I said.

'Yeah, yeah,' said Dad. 'There's a murderer on the loose. Why do you think we're sitting with our backs

187

to the shed, armed to the teeth? Let him try and sneak up on us, that's all.'

'Take that, you fiend!' said Oliver, snapping the pointless shears and missing a tiny fly.

'You really ought to go back to the house,' I said.

'Maybe after elevenses,' said Dad. 'With any luck he'll have come out with his hands in the air by then.'

'Elevenses?'

He dragged a carrier bag from under the bench. It contained half a dozen cans of beer.

'Bit early, even for you two, isn't it?' said Pete.

'We're waiting for half-ten,' said his dad. 'Patiently.' He snapped the shears again – missed another fly. 'God, they're quick,' he said.

Angie jerked her head at Pete and me.

'We should have told them about Smurfit,' I said as we walked away.

'We tried. They didn't want to listen.'

Like I might have said before, there was a lot of stroll space in the grounds of Naffington Hall. There were steps to climb, and walls to jump off, and bushes to push through, and things to amble around, and we did all that, just to keep away from the house and the killer inside it. We were approaching this ancient Greek female with a pot on her shoulder (a statue) when Angie said, 'Of course, we might not be *entirely* safe out here in the open.'

'We'll see the murderer if he comes along,' I said.

'We don't know who he is. It could be anyone.'

'So if we see anyone we make a run for it.'

'He has a gun. He shot Smurfit with it. He could be aiming at us right this minute from behind a bush or from a window in the house.'

We stopped. Stared about us. We saw no one, but if a gun was trained on us from a distance there was no reason why we should.

'The secret garden!' Angie said.

'What about it?' I asked.

'It's not overlooked and it has a high wall. No one would see us in there.'

'They would if they came in.'

'We'll get Pete to lie on the ground with his feet against the door.'

'Good thinking. Come on, Garrett!'

On the way to the secret garden, I said, 'You know, if this was a mystery story instead of real life, everything would mean something.'

'What are you talking about?' Angie said.

'Statues, graves, empty wheelbarrows, secret gardens, they'd all have some significance, or be clues, or be put in to throw the reader off track. Everyone in the story too, they'd all be doing something on the sly or have something in their past that would give them a motive for killing someone.'

'You read too much,' said Pete.

'I do not!' I said. 'I make a point of reading as little as you do. But I know these things.'

'Yeah, well, this isn't a story,' Angie said. 'It's really happening, and here's the door to the secret garden that has no relevance to anything in the known universe, so let's get the other side of it and hide.'

She lifted the latch. The door didn't open.

'It was stiff last time too,' she said. 'Come on, shoulders against it.'

We put our shoulders against the door and pushed. It still wouldn't open.

I indicated the enormous keyhole we'd missed so far. 'Probably locked,' I said.

'It could be bolted on the inside,' said Pete.

'Yes, but to be bolted on the inside there'd have to be someone in there.'

'Who says there isn't?'

'Let's find out,' Angie said.

She raised a fist to hammer the door.

I grabbed her wrist.

She elbowed me in the stomach.

I gasped. Clutched my gut. 'What was that for?'

'You grabbed my wrist.'

'Only to stop you hammering and drawing attention to us. The idea is not to be noticed – remember? That includes not being—'

'What's that?' said Pete suddenly.

'What's what?' said Angie.

'That beeping sound.'

'Beeping s...? Oh, yes.'

Now we all heard it. A tiny but definite *beep-beep-beep, beep-beep-beep.*

'It's coming from Jiggy,' said Pete.

'Me?' I said.

'He's right,' said Angie. She put her head on my chest.

'What are you doing?' I asked.

'Listening to your beep.'

'Is it his heart?' said Pete. 'Wouldn't be surprised. I always knew there was something weird about him. He's an android, isn't he?'

Angie reached into my pocket. Took my pen out.

Beep-beep-beep.

'It's the one Roderick gave you,' she said.

'Yes,' I said. 'But why's it beeping?'

She unscrewed the pen. Inside one half was a tiny battery, which was blinking.

'It's a blinking battery,' I said.

'I think it's a tracking device,' said Angie.

'Tracking device? Why would Roderick give me a tracking device?'

'How about to see where you were at all times? Where we all were.'

'All?'

'The guests. He gave each of us one of these. But *why*, that's what I...' She stopped. Slapped her forehead. 'The tower!'

'Tower?'

'Top of, Friday night, voices in drainpipe. Because of this pen, Roderick knew we were up there and he must have told Honor and Rudy to have that fight for our benefit.'

'You thought we'd been spotted by a spycam in a ciggie packet.'

'I thought wrong. It was this pen. You twonk, McCue.'

'Twonk? That's unfair. How was I to know the pens were tracking devices?'

'You weren't, but I bet only you kept yours. Thanks to you they knew where we were every minute of the day. They must even have known when we went to the village. That's how your mum and Bogart knew when to start their snog. Roderick, orchestrating everything, knew we were coming back to the house and told them to get behind that tree and do the hanky-panky routine. If this battery hadn't started beeping to say it needed replacing we wouldn't have got it even now.'

'OK, but it doesn't matter now, does it? Roderick's not on the case any more. The phoney murders are behind us, even if the real ones aren't.'

'Yes, but I still hate this thing.'

Angie dropped the two bits of pen on the ground and stamped on them hard. I was sorry to see that nice pen pulped, but I had to admit that it was good to have solved one mystery as a team.

'One for all and all for lunch?' I said with a winning smile.

'Say that once more,' Angie said, 'and I'll slug you.'

I dropped the winning smile.

'Er...' said Pete slowly.

'Er what?' I asked.

'Look over there.'

He was gazing across the garden. At a tree. At someone leaning against it. A tall man in a long coat (or a long man in a tall coat – depends how you look at it). The man's face was shadowed by a hat brim pulled very low.

'I think he's watching us,' said Pete.

'Why don't you go and ask him?' I said.

'Why don't you?'

'Because I suggested it.'

'Yeah, but I saw him first.'

'Angie could go,' I said.

'She could stay right here too,' said Ange.

'And don't forget the gun,' said Pete.

'We don't know that he has one,' I said.

'No, but he might have.'

'Mm.'

We could have stood there for quite a while discussing this. We could also have trotted over as a dynamic trio before the man could get his gun out, wrestled him to the ground, torn his hat off, and seen who he was. We could even have linked arms and done the cancan while singing a song that didn't match the situation at all. But we didn't do any of these things.

No. We took another course entirely.

We ran like stink.

'Has he moved?' Angie asked as we hurtled towards the house.

I glanced over my shoulder. 'No. Yes.'

'Which?'

'He's just started.'

'Which way?'

'Which way what?'

'Is he going?'

'This way.'

'This way?'

'After us.'

'What, you mean strolling slowly, hands in pockets, that sort of thing?'

'No, I mean running. Fast.'

'Ooooh!' said Angie.

Pete led the charge. Unusual for him, cos he's no runner. But because he was in the lead he was the first to reach a door. I don't think he was fussy which door it was. Any door would have done as long as it could be opened in front of us and closed behind us. Ange and I weren't too fussy either. When Pete ran up the steps, we weren't a whole lot of miles behind him. Fortunately this door wasn't locked, so we were able to leap in and slam it. It was only when the door was shut that we realised we were in the part of the house the actors had been sleeping in, changing in, and – a couple of them – switching characters in to fool us.

The main room, which we were in, smelled old, a bit damp, kind of musty like a charity shop. A pair of baseball bats hung on the wall, crossed like swords. There wasn't much furniture. The coat rack, the little magazine table, a couple of armchairs, a wardrobe, a desk with a laptop on it, and that was it. The laptop's lid was raised and there was a picture on the screen of a room in the house. The dining room. We were taking all this in when we realised two extra things. The first was that the door we'd come in by was another one without a key. Or a bolt. The second thing was that there were footsteps outside, coming up the steps.

'Quick, against the door!' Angie said.

She leaped towards it – alone. Pete and I had leaped at furniture.

'We could only just keep him out with a pool table,' I said from behind an armchair. 'Without a pool table we don't stand a chance.'

'He's right,' said Pete from behind the wardrobe door he'd opened.

Angie snorted. 'This is obviously *women's* work!'

She seized one of the baseball bats from the wall, raised it over her head and, when the door opened, brought it down hard on the man in the hat, who crumpled to an instant face-down heap.

'Well, that was easy,' I said from behind my chair.

'Is he unconscious?' Pete asked from behind the wardrobe door.

Angie bent over the man. His hat had stayed on even though it had been batted. 'Well, he's not moving.'

'He could be pretending,' said Pete. 'When you get

really close, he'll reach up and strangle you.'

Angie jumped back, out of reach of hands that might jerk up and turn her throat into a drinking straw. Pete and I stepped boldly out from behind the furniture and approached the man on the floor. Not too near.

'Unconscious or not,' I said, 'he's dangerous as long as he's just left there. We ought to tie him up. And gag him.'

'Gag him?' said Ange. 'Jig, whatever your deranged mind tells you, this is not an Enid Blyton. But I agree about tying him up.' She glanced around. 'If we only had some rope...'

'This do?' said Pete, hauling a piece of rope out of the wardrobe.

It was the noose he'd tossed off the roof a pair of nights ago.

Angie took it from him. 'You two,' she said, untying the knot in the rope. 'Stand over him in case he wakes up. Pete, take this.' She handed him the baseball bat. 'Jiggy, you grab the other one. Then both of you get ready to clobber him if he so much as blinks.'

'We won't know if he blinks,' I said. 'He's face down.'

'All right, if he twitches.'

I took the second bat off the wall and Pete and I went closer to the man on the floor and stood on each side of him, bats half raised, ready for anything. Well, almost anything. When a pigeon cooed outside we almost threw our bats in the air and ran out clutching our hair.

'Hey, look,' said Pete while Angie was tying the man's hands behind him.

'I'm busy,' said Ange.

But I wasn't. I looked. Pete had seen something hanging in the wardrobe. A police sergeant's uniform.

'You don't think…' I said.

'Bit of a coincidence if not,' said Pete.

'There, done,' said Ange, finishing the rope work.

'I hope that's a good knot,' I said.

'It's a terrific knot. A triple. He'd need a knife to get free.'

'He might have a knife. He is a murderer.'

'Well, it won't do him much good with his hands tied behind him. Let's turn him over and see who he is.'

'What about the uniform?' asked Pete.

'Uniform?' said Ange.

She looked to where he pointed. The wardrobe. And stared.

'You don't think…'

'That's what I said,' I said.

'But if that's Sergeant Fawkes' uniform…'

'If that's Sergeant Fawkes' uniform,' said Pete, 'he must have been acting too.'

'Unless he was killed and the man in the hat took his uniform and hung it there,' I said. 'We can ask him about that when he comes to.'

'Not if he's gagged,' said Ange.

'He's not gagged.'

'No, but you said he should be. If we gag him and ask him about the sergeant's uniform, he won't be able to answer.'

'OK, don't gag him. Turn him over.'

'Me?' she said, eyes widening.

'Of course you,' I said. 'Turning over unconscious murderers in hats is one of those things I just *know* that you would do really well. Besides, we're holding the bats. We might need to bash him after he's killed you.'

So she rolled him over onto his back, and...

'Holy murder weekends,' she said, staring at the face attached to the head beneath the hat.

Pete and I also stared at the face – speechlessly.

It belonged to Roderick Basket-Case.

Who was supposed to be dead.

CHAPTER EIGHTEEN

It took us a minute. Maybe it shouldn't have taken that long, but the one person apart from our parents that we hadn't suspected of being the Naffington Hall murderer was the first one to be really murdered. Really murdered? Well, he obviously hadn't been. So what was going on here?

'We didn't actually see his body, did we?' I said.

Angie shook her head – 'No' – and nodded the same head in the direction of the wardrobe. 'Any more than we saw proof that Sergeant Fawkes was a real sergeant.'

'If the sergeant was an actor,' I said, 'and Rod here was just *pretending* to have been killed...'

Wherever this thought was going I didn't get to it, because of the siren.

The police siren.

In the room with us.

Angie and I whirled round. Stared at the laptop on the desk, which Pete was leaning over. 'Sound relay system,' he said over the siren. 'Pumps pre-recorded sounds to remote speakers.' He touched a key and the siren stopped. 'My dad used to have one a bit like this. The external sound's muted at present, but I could send it to any outlet that's set up to receive it.' He stabbed another button. The image on the laptop changed to the courtyard in front of the house, where the cars were parked. 'Like there. Shall I?'

'No!' Angie said sharply.

'Oh, come on. Make 'em jump.'

'No. Do that and those of them who know about this would know where we are.'

'So? Do we care?'

'Not sure. Maybe. You know what this means, don't you? Means there was no police car.'

'There wouldn't have to be if the sergeant was a fraud,' I said.

'Right. Doesn't happen to be an ambulance siren too, does there?' she asked Pete.

Pete pressed more keys. The first produced gentle birdsong, the second a clap of thunder so loud that all three of us left our shoes. A third button produced the sound of an approaching ambulance.

'So,' Angie said. 'No ambulance either.'

'They bundled us into the dining room so we'd *imagine* them taking Roderick's body away,' I said.

'Which we did, after they'd convinced us they were telling the truth for once.'

'And the thunder,' Angie said. 'Remember last night, Jig? Big storm, but when we went onto the roof it was only raining? The thunder sound must have been sent from here, like the sirens.'

'Wonder what this does?' Pete said.

He was leaning over a little black box with a glass dome on the side. He flipped a switch on the box.

FLASH!

I staggered blindly and sensed Angie staggering just as blindly nearby.

'Cool,' said Pete.

'Cool?' I said. 'I can't see a thing!'

'Me neither,' said Angie.

'This box must generate lightning outside when sensors are activated,' Pete said. 'Same principle as the sound relay thing, but visual.'

'Technology,' said Angie, blinking wildly. 'I hate it.'

'I love it,' said Pete, and tripped the flasher again, blinding us once more.

Angie reached out to smack his head, but missed. 'Do that again, Garrett,' she said, 'and—'

He flashed her a third time and ducked another blind swipe.

When we finally got our sight back, I noticed

something moving on the laptop screen. 'Hey, it's live,' I said. 'I thought they were just pictures.'

The moving thing was the car that had just drawn up in the courtyard. We watched as a man got out of it.

'Sergeant Fawkes is in plain clothes!' said Angie.

I whistled softly. 'And not *only* Sergeant Fawkes...'

'What do you mean?'

'I've just realised where else I've seen him. In Haddenuff, lifting trays out of a catering van.'

'Are there any other views?' Angie asked Pete.

He did some keyboard stuff and the onscreen images changed in quick succession. As well as the courtyard and the dining room we saw the library, the upstairs landing, the view from the back of the house (with Dad and Ollie on the bench with the rake and broken shears), and finally the main hall full of Golden Oldies.

'The bedrooms and the attic?' Angie asked.

'No, this is it,' said Pete.

'Well, that's something.'

The man who'd played Sergeant Fawkes had entered the hall and was being introduced by Gerald Tozer.

'Any sound?' I asked Pete.

He pressed a button and we heard the tail end of

Gerald Tozer introducing the newcomer to the Prossers and Audrey.

'– is Bernard,' he said.

'You didn't have much of a part,' said Audrey.

'I run the company that provides the food here,' Bernard said. 'I always fancied acting and Mr Basket-Case was kind enough to give me a small role – my first ever, since school. How'd I do?'

'You made a very convincing policeman,' said Honor Naffington, as was.

'I can't get over this,' said Belinda Prosser. 'I really believed it. All of it. Talk about a wedding present to remember!'

'Yes,' said Billy, who looked like he didn't know whether to laugh or kill someone. 'I look forward to telling my next wife all about it.'

'Just wait till I see Uncle Roderick,' Belinda giggled stupidly.

'I thought he would've been here by now,' said another voice. 'Wonder where he's got to?'

And DCI Smurfit stepped into shot wiping fake blood from her forehead.

'We have been *so* conned,' said Angie, in the room with me and Pete. 'Set up twice in two days. Fell for it – twice!'

'So now you know everything,' said another voice.

204

We jumped round. Roderick, still on the floor with his hands behind him, had his eyes open. 'I imagine one of you clobbered me?' he said.

'What, us?' said Angie. 'No, you tripped and banged your head as you came in.'

'So why are my hands fastened behind me?'

'We thought you were a murderer.'

'You were meant to.'

'You were the man in the hat all along?'

'Of course.' Roderick chuckled, then winced. 'The old head's pounding. Do the decent thing and release me, eh?'

'Why were you chasing us just now?' Angie said.

'I wasn't chasing you. Well, not really. I was going to fess up.'

'Fess up?'

'Admit everything. I thought you should hear it from the horse's mouth, me being the horse that's been bugging you so much.'

'Bugging us,' said Angie. She narrowed her eyes at me. 'Oh, you've been doing that all right.'

'So if you would just untie me…?' he said.

I started forward to do just that, but Angie flung an arm across my chest.

'I want some answers first.'

'Answers?'

'To questions such as were our parents in on the supposedly real murders deal? Yours and Smurfit's.'

'Well, Peg knew, being one of the Players, but the other three didn't, any more than Belinda and Billy did. My murder and DCI Smurfit's are an additional ingredient that I plan to build into the weekends when we launch commercially in the autumn.'

'So all the effort we put in to working out who killed Sir Duff, Honor and Bogart was a waste of time,' Angie said.

Roderick chuckled again. 'A stratagem to get you involved, that's all. A warm-up of sorts. Ultimately, of course, it didn't matter whether or not you associated the name of the flower with Gerald because the "real" murders would soon have put such shenanigans in the shade.'

He must have realised from our silent glares that he hadn't won us over yet, because he went on.

'Look, everyone knows what happens at murder weekends. Actors play assorted characters, pretend to be either killers or victims, but no one's really hurt and everyone has a jolly time. Admittedly, my plan to introduce a couple of "actual" murders and an "actual" police officer turns things a shade darker, but only for one night. In the morning, once the shock of finding the second victim has worn off, all is revealed and everyone has a good old laugh.'

'What about the dead phone lines and the mobile signal shortage?' Pete asked. 'Were they down to you?'

'Oh, indeed. Such things are easily managed. Now can I *please* get up?'

Angie looked at me. 'What do you think, Jig? Set him free or let him rot here forever and a day?'

I didn't answer. I heard her, but I was looking at my feet. There was nothing wrong with my feet, but I was getting an idea, and you have to look somewhere when an idea's coming, and feet are as good a place as any.

'Jig?' Angie said.

I lifted my eyes from my fascinating hooves. 'I'm getting a thought,' I said.

'Well, fight it,' she said. 'This is not a time for thoughts.'

'You might like this one,' I said.

'Oh, go on then.'

'Over here. Pete. You too.'

They trailed me to a corner of the room, where we went into a huddled confab. 'What I'm thinking,' I began, 'is that lessons need to be taught here.'

'Lessons?' Pete said. 'I hate lessons.'

'Not to us, you plank. To them.'

'Who?'

'The people who've taken us for such a ride this weekend.'

'What sort of lessons do you have in mind?' Angie asked.

'Well, just one lesson really. A murderous one.'

I told them the plan that had come to me while I was staring at my trotters. As they heard me out, smiles spread slowly across their lip areas.

'They'll never go along with it,' Angie said when I'd finished.

'I think they will,' I said. 'They're pretty anti about all this.'

Pete grinned. 'Let's ask 'em.'

I turned to Roderick. 'Where do you keep the fake blood you use when people get shot or thrown off roofs?'

'There are a couple of bottles in the desk,' he said. 'Why?'

I didn't say. Just went to the desk and took a little bottle of red stuff from a drawer. 'Anything we can use as a gag?' I asked next.

'A gag? You mean as in joke?'

'No, not as in joke. There've been enough of those, at our expense anyway.'

He found out what I meant when I took a silk scarf

from the coat rack and gave it to Angie to loop around his mouth and fasten at the back of his neck in a big fat girly bow. Roderick was still on the floor, hands tied behind him, when we left a minute later to go and see what the dads thought of my fiendish plan to get back at The Pure Isle Players.

CHAPTER NINETEEN

We should have been actors ourselves. You should have seen us. Heard us. When we sauntered back into the house after talking to my dad and Oliver and saw DCI Smurfit alive and well, our mouths dropped open in total shock.

'But you're...you're...'

'Dead?' laughed the woman who'd played Smurfit and Myrtle the maid.

'But...but...' we stammered, gasping for words.

'Jane's not the police,' Reg Mote said. 'She works in a bank.'

'A bank?'

'You've been had,' my treacherous mother chortled.

Then they explained, like we didn't already know, that Bernard the caterer wasn't in the police either, and that Roderick wasn't dead.

'Roderick isn't dead? But...they took his body away!'

Now everyone was laughing. Even Billy Prosser cracked a grin. The three of us just stood there, bewildered, disbelieving.

'He should be along any minute,' said Lady Helga. 'He's had to keep well out of it since last night to avoid being spotted.'

'I said a nice juicy murder or two would take your minds off the exams, didn't I?' my mother said.

'You did,' I said. 'We could be in therapy for years thanks to you.'

'Oh, no. You'll look back on this weekend and have a right old chuckle. I know you will.'

'Yeah, we'll do a lot of chuckling in our straitjackets.'

We asked all the questions we already had answers to, and gradually allowed ourselves the odd smile and 'Yes, well, I guess it does have its funny side,' and before long we were making a show of reluctantly admitting that it had been a weekend to remember. But then – suddenly – the front door was flung back and Pete's dad, Oliver, stood on the threshold looking like his hair was about to take off.

'It's Mel!' he said, ultra-dramatically. 'He's dead!'

The laughter tailed off.

'What?' said my mother.

Oliver stared at her, all bug-eyed. 'Mel! Roderick's killed him!' We believed he'd been carted off to the body shop, but he must have faked the whole thing, and we saw him, and Mel was really peed off that we'd been stitched up, and he started having a go, and

211

things got kind of heated, I mean *very* heated, and—'

'Slow down, slow down,' Audrey said, touching his arm to calm him.

Ollie took a breath. A ragged one. Everyone was still smiling, like his performance was part of the weekend, but when he tottered past Audrey like his knees were turning to rubber and continued ranting like a half-mad person, the smiles started to shrink.

'Mel grabbed Roderick by the shirt and threatened to do him some damage – you know how he overreacts sometimes, Peg – and Roderick grabbed these garden shears and warned him to take it easy, but Mel was so out of it by this time that he didn't let up for a minute, and...' – he sobbed at this point, which could have blown it, but didn't – 'and then Roderick lost it too, sort of panicked I guess, and drove the shears into Mel's chest. Right in. Straight into Mel's heart. Then he ran off.'

'Mel ran off?' said my mother.

'No, *Roderick*,' Ollie snapped. 'He could be miles away by now – miles. He...he murdered my friend!'

'My dad's *dead*?' I said, like it was only just starting to sink in.

Angie gave me a warning look that said, 'Low-key, Jig, low-key.'

'I'm afraid so, Jig,' said Ollie. 'And Peg, I'm so sorry.

There was nothing I could do. It was all over so...so...'

He stopped like he couldn't go on. Just stood there, all wild-eyed and twitchy. None of his listeners were smiling now. The colour had drained from the cheeks of some, especially my mother's.

'This is quite a thing to take in,' said Gerald Tozer, who didn't look as convinced as the rest. 'You'd better show us, old chap.'

Oliver whirled on him fiercely. 'Show you? *Show* you? You think I'm making it up? A murder's been committed, you moron! An actual bloody *murder*!'

'Yes, old fellow, yes, I hear you,' Gerald said, stepping back a pace, 'but we need to see for ourselves. Weekend like this, you know, well, kind of hard to take anything seriously when you know what's been going on behind the scenes.'

Jane, the bank worker who'd kidded us that she was a maid and a detective chief inspector, stepped forward. 'Will you take us to where it happened?' she asked Oliver in a quiet, concerned, worried little voice.

He made a big effort. 'Take you,' he said, breathing hard. 'Yes, right, but...' He sounded like he was about to break down, but made a superhuman effort to hold it together. 'This way then, this way.'

He rushed out like he was being chased by a red-eyed hound that wanted a slice of his backside. The

213

others went after him. The mums went last. Mine told us to stay where we were. She looked genuinely rattled now.

When we were alone, Angie said, 'I didn't know Ollie had it in him.'

'I hope your dad can be as convincing,' Pete said to me.

'Even if he isn't,' I said, 'my mother might need a stress break after this. Maybe not a murder weekend, though.'

We laughed quite a bit about that.

We went after the adults, but kept well out of sight behind them. Oliver led the way to the potting shed where, on the ground beside the bench, lay my dad, absolutely still. The garden shears that Ollie had been failing to slice insects with were also there – standing to attention in my dad's chest. Anyone who didn't know that the sharp ends had been snapped off would automatically believe that the blades were buried about midway between his nipples. I don't know how they'd rigged that, but it was a work of genius. And there was a lot of blood. Fake blood, naturally, but Dad's shirt looked ruined.

Angie nodded approvingly. 'He seems to be handling it.'

'It's all that relaxation therapy,' I said. 'When he's

doing his exercises it looks like he's not breathing. Like now.'

The dads hadn't needed much persuading to go along with my big revenge plan. They'd been as mad as hell when they heard Roderick was still alive. Not mad that he wasn't dead exactly, only that he'd screwed them so totally. By the time they'd heard the full story they'd been even keener than we were to get even.

'You'll get a month's worth of mouthfuls from Mum if you pull it off,' I'd warned my father.

He'd grinned meanly. 'She'll get a month's worth from me for not filling me in on the fake death of Roderick scenario.'

'My mum won't be tremendously pleased with you either,' Angie had said to Oliver.

He'd grinned too. His eyes had been glittering. 'It'll be worth it.'

The sight of Dad lying there so still and bloody clinched it for everyone. My mother dropped to her knees, wailing hysterically, and everyone else looked stunned and horrified – even Gerald – glancing about like they expected Roderick to leap out from something, wielding a deadly watering can or trowel.

'How long do you think your dad'll be able to keep it up?' Angie whispered from the bush we were crouching behind.

I shrugged. 'Knowing him, he'll milk it to bits. Hold his breath at least until my mother's ordered a wreath.'

'Do we have to stick around?' Pete asked.

'You mean behind this bush?' Angie said.

'No, not behind this bush. It's village fete day in Haddenuff.'

'I thought you thought village fetes were naff.'

'They are. But I need a break from all this phoney murder rubbish.'

'We'd have to tell the Golden Oldies we were going.'

'We didn't yesterday.'

'They didn't have a father's corpse on their hands yesterday.'

'They haven't today,' I said. 'They just think they have. We could leave them a note.'

'A note?'

'We put it inside the piano, and when we get back we say we hid it as part of the murder weekend and shake our heads sadly about how dumb they are for not finding it.'

It was agreed. We scribbled a quick note to say that we'd gone to the village, laid it on the piano keys, put the lid down, and left the house.

It was a grey day. Cloud everywhere, mainly above us. But we were in high spirits as we scurried up the drive.

'Pretty neat end to a lousy weekend, eh?' I said.

'There'll be trouble later, though,' said Ange.

'Yeah. But let's enjoy the moment.'

'What about Roderick?' said Pete.

'What about him?' Angie said.

'Well, he's tied up and gagged and no one knows he's there.'

'We'll set him free when we get back if no one's found him. Maybe.'

'Hey, I just remembered,' Pete said.

'What?'

'The flyer from the fete said there'd be a fish and chip van.'

'Bit early for fish and chips,' I said.

'Yeah, but we missed breakfast.'

'You'd seriously have fish and chips for breakfast?'

'Not fish. But chips, absolutely.'

'I don't suppose it would hurt this once,' Angie said. Then she laughed. 'Murder and chips. Perfect combination.'

I smiled. 'One for all and all for chips?'

They stopped walking abruptly. Both of them. Which made me stop too. They were looking at me, kind of sadly.

'What?' I said.

'Jig,' said Angie. 'We've been talking.'

'Who has?'

'Me and Pete.'

'What, without me?'

'Yes.'

I had a sudden sense of foreboding.

'And?' I said.

'It's time,' said Pete.

'For what?' I said.

'To kill it,' said Ange.

'Kill it? Kill what?'

'The Musketeer deal,' said Pete.

'The "one for all and all for lunch" deal,' said Ange.

'You mean...?' I said.

'Yes,' they said.

'We're too old,' said Pete.

'We've outgrown it,' said Angie.

'I haven't,' I said.

'Well, we have,' said Pete.

They started walking again.

'No, wait,' I said.

They didn't wait. Didn't even look back. I couldn't get my head around this. No more Musketeers? No more us against the world, shoulder to shoulder, back to back, toe to toe?

It was a sad day.

The end of an era.

But then the sun kicked a hole in the clouds and a bird started to sing, and I thought, Hey, sunshine, bird singing, I've survived a murder weekend and I'm off to a village fete to have chips for breakfast with my lifelong buds. Things could be worse.

Couldn't they?

You have to think that way when your whole life's just turned to dust.

Well, you do if you're like me.

If your name's...

Jiggy McCue

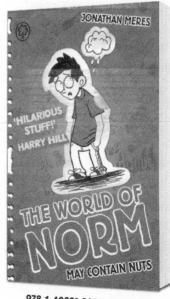